To Handcuff Lightning

SHARON KD HOSKINS

ISBN-13: 978-0-9794576-2-3

For Alberta, Viola, and Effie Naomi "Honey"

*To handcuff lightning, put a hold on thunder, run through
the graveyard, and put the dead to wonder.*

Willie Lee Clover, 1921–1992

To Handcuff Lightning
Clover Family Series
(Book One)

ONE

"'When I get some age on me, I'm gonna have me a beer.' That's the first thing Screamie said to me," says Algie as she sets a plate of hot food in front of Benny Thomas, the bar owner from across the street. "Before that Benny, It was a whole lot of screaming or no sound at all!"

It's October 1957 in Dayton, Ohio. Algie Julia Jordan-Clover is the owner of The Place, a small restaurant on Dayton's west side at the corner of Germantown and Hawthorn Streets. Three-year-old Screamie is the daughter of Early Bird, Algie's boyfriend. When she first met the little girl, the child let out her signature loud, dry wail that belied her tiny size. Algie's reply was to reach down and place a small piece of cornbread into her open mouth. "She can't holler if her mouth is full." Early told Algie that people prefer to use his daughter's nickname since it's easier to pronounce than her real name, Máxke[1].

Nowadays, the little girl with the pale, yellow-red complexion and fine, sandy hair that sprouts from her head like a veil of gauze is a regular guest at The Place. Screamie's lithe body is as fragile as her hair. Algie easily lifts and cradles her several times a day; showering her with kisses and caressing her soft, unruly hair.

---

[1] Máxke (mah-SKI') is a Delaware Indian (Ohio tribe) word that means red.

During the week, Screamie is with her mother and three other siblings; each having different fathers. But on weekends she eats, sleeps, and plays with a doll that is more raggedy than Ann, on a mat next to Algie's stool behind the restaurant's counter. She rarely screams now. Instead, the talkative toddler strings isolated words — she's heard overhead — into nonsensical phrases that amuse both Algie and the restaurant's patrons.

"Early around?" asks Benny.

"Yes. He's next door at Crook's.

Benny looks directly at Algie, and before he loses his nerve, goes ahead with the question he's wanted to ask her. "How does that child's mother feel about you keeping her all the time?"
Algie sets a bowl of peach cobbler in front of the customer next to Benny, and walks back into the kitchen for the next order without a word.

"Oh, crap," he mutters to himself. "That's too much, too soon, Benny. You've blown it now."

She soon returns from the kitchen with a paper plate wrapped in aluminum foil and hands it to the waiting customer at the open end of the lunch counter. She next takes the coffeepot from the burner and refills Benny's mug. Without looking up at him, she finally says, "You know, she came in here once. Just stood there and stared at me from across the counter; then turned around and walked right back out."

"What did you do then?"

"I told Early about it and he confronted her. She told him she just wanted to see what I looked like. She heard I had three grown daughters, so at least I know how to deal with girls. It doesn't bother her that Screamie is here because she's got three other kids at home."

"Algie, how do you feel about it? After all, she's right, your girls are grown."

"Screamie's no bother and none of my girls have kids yet. I really enjoy having the baby girl around."

Benny watches the heat rising from his coffee for a minute and takes a sip. Shifting gears, he switches the conversation to a less sensitive subject. "How long now has this spot been a restaurant? Is it three or four years?"

"It's been five years. And prayer and hard work is what got it done. Besides, a restaurant is a much better place for me and my daughters than a pawn shop; especially with their Daddy gone now." Benny nods sympathetically. He had stopped by the pawn shop often to chat with Algie, even when her husband was still alive. He now eats lunch and dinner at her restaurant every day, except Sunday when his bar is closed, and Monday when The Place is closed.

Benny was shocked to learn Algie had taken up with Early, a day laborer who doesn't know where his next dollar is coming from. He had thought she would prefer his reserved, slow style. But he hasn't given up yet.

Algie looks younger than her 48 years and Early looks older than his 33. Therefore, few people suspect there is any age difference between them. Her petite size of 4'11" and 110 pounds also helps camouflage her age. She never wears make-up on her unblemished, heart-shaped face. And, only short, tiny lines have started to emerge across her forehead and around the corners of her mouth. The dark, large pupils of Algie's eyes are stark still. Like a doll's stare, her eyes leave some people uncomfortable, while others are hypnotized. Her lips are puckered into a permanent kiss. Each morning she moistens them with petroleum jelly to counter their propensity for dryness; a condition that makes her subconsciously lick her lips.

Algie's lightly salted, thick, black hair is pulled into a ponytail tied with a fat rubber band; the waist-length coils swinging freely across her back. During the course of the day, wayward strands eventually float out of the band creating a halo around her head.

Algie was not initially attracted to Early. Tall and straight, Early's body is a long, lean column of shiny bronze copper. His short, straight teeth are filed down to perfect white squares and his almond-shaped eyes are like narrow slits. He's balding, but still has a thick bush of hair atop his head. He first came into The Place because he was cold standing on the corner waiting for a job. He had immediately liked Algie because she was pretty, friendly, and didn't ask too many questions. Soon he began making it a habit to come in for coffee, even when it wasn't cold. If he didn't get picked for a job, he'd sit at the counter all morning, drinking coffee and talking.

Early told Algie about his military time in Korea, the reason his mother named him Early (he was born a week before his due date at 3:00 AM), and all about his daughter, Screamie. Early talked about his family in Texas and the reason why he decided to move to Ohio after he got out of the service.

Eventually, he asked Algie if his mail could come to The Place because his military service checks would sometimes go missing from the rooming house where he lives on South Euclid Avenue. He then begin showing up on weekends with Screamie. They've never been on a date, but everyone knows Algie and Early are a couple. He eats all his meals, for free, at The Place and turns over most of his daily wages to Algie. When she initially refused the money he explained, "I just need a little walking around money in my pocket. The rest is for you." Algie opens his mail and even signs and cashes his checks. She gives him his rent money and he lets her know of any additional expenses he might have, such as money demands from Screamie's mother.

Periodically, Early's mother will send a letter and Algie reads it to him. His mother's writing is more scrawl than script, but not much different from Algie's own mother, Chauncey. Early quit school in the 6th grade and admits, "I couldn't read or write that good when I was in school and it's worse now!" After reading the letters from Texas, Algie asks Early how he would like to answer. She jots down a short note, summarizing his response, and folds a couple of dollars into the envelopes before mailing them.

Algie's daughters have not questioned their mother about her relationship with Early. The only time the couple is together is at The Place. He's never been to the house and their mother has never gone on a date with him. They reason the relationship is purely platonic. Besides, Early is nothing like their father. Edward "Eddie Mack" Clover had broad shoulders and muscular arms shaped and sculpted by years of farm labor that began when he was 10 years old. His vanilla skin was dotted with tiny red freckles from head-to-toe and his sunset red hair was locked into tight curls, each with its own unique cowlick.

He got his green-hazel eyes from a white mother who left him with his paternal grandmother the day he was born and never returned. His father, Gabriel Clover left him, too—got himself killed before Eddie Mack's first birthday.

In Dublin, Eddie Mack had a reputation as a dependable, able-bodied man who took care of his family and didn't owe anybody a thing — not even a favor. Both women and men were drawn to his always present and genuine smile.

When Eddie Mack first came to call on Algie, Chauncey tore into him with a relentless verbal attack. "No, he could not call on her daughter. No, he could not take her daughter on a picnic. No, he could not walk her daughter home from church."

Through it all, Eddie Mack just smiled — not at Chauncey — but directly at Algie. Three months later, at dawn, he silently rolled his truck into Algie's front yard. She was standing in the open doorway, waiting. Eddie Mack took her hand and led Algie to his truck. When they returned the next day, they were married. She was 17; he was 21.

Several Clover family members had already migrated north before Eddie Mack and Algie arrived in Dayton on September 14, 1950, with Chauncey and their three daughters; Tressie, Viola, and Honey. Algie was not convinced the move was the right thing for her family. She expressed her concern to Edward (she never called him Eddie Mack) every single day of the weeks and months leading up to their departure. That day finally came and without complaint, Algie helped load their belongings into the used 1950 Buick sedan bought specifically for the 11-hour car ride to Ohio.

Eddie Mack's cousin, Willie "Crook" Clover, had found a house for them to rent. Eddie Mack soon found work at Dessi Airplane Parts, while Algie took a job at the pawn shop which was only a 10-minute walk from their house and next door to Crook's business, Clover's Pool Room. Six months after she began working there as a clerk, the owner of the pawn shop decided to move back home to St. Louis. Eddie Mack seized the opportunity. They would transform the pawn shop into a restaurant. He would keep his job at Dessi, but grow vegetables in their backyard and build the wooden tables and chairs — just like he did back home.

The idea of a restaurant appealed to Algie, too, since she is better at cooking then haggling with pawn shop clientele. Four days after they took over the payments for the pawn shop, Eddie Mack dropped dead at Dessi from an aneurysm. Overwhelmed by grief, shock, and the reality of suddenly becoming a single parent, Algie immediately began making plans to return home to Georgia, as Chauncey urged her to do.

However, her daughters had other plans. Back in Georgia, they had pleaded with their parents to move north and give them a chance for a life doing anything but sharecropping. Viola, the middle girl, begin the argument by reminding her mother of that fact, "I am not going back to slave farming. I will be eighteen on my next birthday and I can get a job anywhere. I'm staying here!"

Algie did want a better life for her girls and it was true, there wasn't much opportunity for them back in Dublin. She decided to let the Bible make the decision; not her fears, not her daughters' youthful determination, not Chauncey's relentless nagging, and not Crook's doomsday predictions.

Ten days after she laid her husband of 20 years to rest in Greencastle Cemetery (she couldn't afford to take him back home for burial), Algie laid her right hand on her grandmother Julia's bible and prayed for God to show her the way. Just as her grandmother had taught her, that night, she slept with the bible underneath her pillow. As soon as she opened her eyes the next morning, she opened the Bible and read the first scripture her eyes focused on:

> "Do not be afraid, for I am with you.
> Do not be anxious, for I am your God.
> I will fortify you, yes, I will help you,
> I will really hold on to you with my right hand of righteousness."[2]

Algie closed the bible and stayed.

With the loss of Edward's income, however, she had to start out by serving lunches right next to the moldy, fake fur coats;

---

[2] *New World Translation of the Bible*, Isaiah 41:10

tarnished "gold" watches; and other assorted pawned goods. She prepared the food at home and used a hot plate to keep it warm at the shop. Five years later, the transformation was complete. In the beginning, all of her daughters helped out at The Place, but now, only Tressie, the eldest, works there full-time.

Benny has finished his lunch and tells Algie he'll see her for dinner. She waves good-bye to him and picks up the newspaper at the end of the counter. Tressie brings the newspaper with her when she comes in the morning, and its left there, all-day, for anyone who wants to read it. It's the second time that Algie has browsed the headlines and, again, nothing in particular catches her eye. She then decides to go check on Chauncey at home, a trip she makes 4–5 times a day.

The 10-minute walk from The Place to the house takes Algie onto Germantown Street for just 1 block. She turns right on Fitch Street, passes five houses, and then turns left onto Dunbar Avenue. There are only eight homes on Dunbar (four on each side of the street). Algie's house is the last one on the left, 246 Dunbar Avenue. The dead end street stops at a brick wall barrier that's about waist high to the average man. A narrow strip of grass separates Algie's house from the wall.

Down a short, but steep hill on the other side of the wall is a parking lot full of yellow cabs owned by the Westside Cab Company. In the center of the sea of cabs is the dispatcher's office; a wooden stall the size of a telephone booth. Cabbies often climb back and forth over the wall to Algie's house to place orders with Chauncey, who recites them to Algie when she checks-in at home.

When Edward and Algie first saw this house, Algie tried, but failed, to hide her disappointment. She wasn't expecting a mansion, but at least their home in Dublin sat on four acres with nobody else's windows peering into theirs. Viola and Honey still live with her, but Tressie is married now.

On the weekends, Algie takes Screamie with her during her trips home. She's tried leaving her at the house with Chauncey, but the little girl refuses to stay. "All the little red thing does is scream all the time anyway," complains Chauncey. "No tears. Just screaming. I don't want to keep her no way."

As her feet instinctively walk toward the house, Algie's mind is seduced by the coolness of the fall day. Back home its harvest time and her favorite crops are in season: beans, onions, peaches, peppers, squash, and pumpkins. She can see the fields like a beloved painting — row upon row of God's bounty framed by a turquoise blue sky; brilliant sunlight; and splashes of red, orange, and yellow spreading across the trees.

Algie sighs and it echoes deep within her. She doesn't regret her decision to stay, but it will never be home. Much too soon, she reaches the house and lets go of the fields of Dublin.

Six, steep steps lead up to the long porch of the house, which has two doorways. The door to the immediate left is always kept locked. Straight ahead, across the length of the porch, is the unlocked door that opens into the living room. Sitting in the middle of the room is a large, coal burning stove. There have been a couple of cool nights this October, but no fire has been lit yet.

Directly behind the stove are two large windows nailed shut and obscured by heavy, white lace curtains. The curtains are discolored from constant exposure to the stove's ash and smoke and, despite repeated washing; they will never be bright, white again.

Opposite the furnace is a long sofa that is flush with the wall. In front of the sofa is an oblong, pecan wood, cocktail table with straight, square legs that have been painted white. In the corner, next to the sofa, there's a tall, floor lamp with an umbra shade shaped like a Chinese lantern. On the other side of the sofa is a single, round table. The only telephone in the house is sitting on it.

To the left of the furnace is an old lowboy with a radio placed on the top shelf. Edward got the radio when somebody discarded or dropped it on the corner of Fitch and Dunbar. The radio is always on, but depending on the time of day, music may or may not be heard since the frequency is in a constant state of flux. Only Honey bothers with it. As soon as she enters the house, she begins turning the wheel up-and-down the dial until she picks up her favorite dance station or radio DJ, Delilah[3].

Chauncey's chair is on the right side of the furnace. Behind her chair is the door that leads to the kitchen. It's a boxcar-shaped room with just enough space for a stove, refrigerator, and a single sink on one side. On the other side, there's a round table with a cork top and two wooden chairs placed side-by-side.

Behind the living room wall is the master bedroom, which is the length of this room and the kitchen combined. The bedroom is accessed via a set of French doors. The beds are sectioned off by makeshift partitions created by king-sized sheets hung over clotheslines. Each section contains a bed. Twin-size beds are in the first two sections and a double bed is in the third section. There is a single door on each side of the room. The bathroom is on the left, the closet on the right. Algie sleeps in the twin bed nearest the bathroom. Chauncey has the middle bed and Honey and Viola share the double bed.

Chauncey is nodding in her chair, mouth full of snuff, but wakes upon hearing Algie enter the house.

"Any cab orders, Mom?"

---

[3] Edythe "Delilah" Lewis was the first African American woman disc jockey in Dayton, Ohio.

"I got two."

Algie is Chauncey's only living child. The three baby girls, before Algie, died within days, and a dead brother, after Algie, lived just two months. "Satan is busy," explained Chauncey, whenever Algie inquired about her dead siblings. Algie's father, Berry Smith, was married to another woman, so Algie was given the last name of her mother's husband, Willie Jordan. Berry also fathered Algie's dead brother, who had been named for both men, Berry Willie Jordan. Algie never knew how her stepfather, Willie, felt about all of this; he never said anything about it. As for Berry, he didn't deny her, but he didn't claim her either. He had 14 other children with a wife to whom he remained married.

When she was older, Algie reasoned that maybe her mother felt her chances of having "live" babies would be better with another man. Chauncey's own mother, Grandma Julia, said as much, accusing her daughter of deliberately pursuing Berry because he had successfully fathered so many children, while the three she had with Willie perished. Soon after her son died, Chauncey left Willie. She could no longer blame him for making "half-done babies" since her second child with Berry had also died.

Chauncey didn't want to leave Georgia, but she couldn't live apart from Algie. She hates Dayton, the house, and The Place most of all. She never goes to "that hole-in-the-wall", choosing instead to prepare and eat all her meals at the house, alone. She ventures outside occasionally to sit on the front porch, but most of the time she passes the day in the sitting room, squatting in a bamboo chair on an overstuffed cushion. Next to the chair is a large spittoon into which she spits the liquefied snuff she constantly chews. The only time the smokeless tobacco leaves her mouth is while she's eating her meals. She drinks her coffee right over it.

The French doors that lead to the sitting room are closed and locked.

In the bedroom, Algie changes her shoes because the ones she had on got wet this morning in the rain. She soon returns to the sitting room and her mother recites the orders from two cabbies, George and Caleb. Algie takes a seat on the couch across from her mother, leans back into the cushions, and closes her eyes. Chauncey, however, is now fully awake and wants to talk. "You busy down there?"

Without moving a muscle, Algie replies, "Not yet. It's Friday, payday; so it will pick up soon."

Algie rents her space for The Place from Mr. Frisch. In fact, Frisch owns the entire building; four sides of fading, crumbling red brick with a flat, tar roof. Frisch has been buying and leasing storefronts on Dayton's Westside since the 1940s. The single level building has three units. The Place is at one end; The House of Faith at the opposite end; and, Clover's Pool Room is in the middle. Algie has never missed a payment, so there's no need for Frisch to make unwelcomed or unannounced visits to her restaurant. However, he makes frequent visits to Crook's place to collect late rent money.

A rotund, bald, white man who rolls up his sleeves and uses suspenders instead of a belt, Frisch doesn't patronize any of the businesses he leases. He just collects the rent and eventually takes care of any repairs the buildings might need. He knows Miss Algie and Crook are related, but she's made it clear the two businesses are run independently, so there's no need for him to question her about Crook's overdue rent or any other goings-on.

The single, wooden front door of The Place is painted dark green and framed on either side by two large picture windows. Honey painted the words, "THE PLACE", in large, bold red, block letters on each window pane. The Place has a long counter with six bar stools; chrome with red plastic seat cushions filled with silver glitter. All the stools have rips and tears patched with silver duct tape, except for the stool Algie reserves for herself behind the counter. On a low shelf, anchored to the wall behind the counter, is a double-burner hot plate; each with a carafe sitting on it. One carafe is full of coffee, the other hot water. Mounted on the wall, next to the carafes, is the telephone and a coat rack is stationed to the immediate left of the door.

The eight, round wood tables in the dining area are covered with forest green, plastic tablecloths. Each table has four chairs with intricately carved designs on the legs and rail back. The chairs were obtained at a foreclosure sale and once anchored an expensive dining room suite, but the rich walnut finish is now distressed. A couple of the tables sway on uneven legs and some of the chairs rock, too. But the furniture is in usable condition and is always clean.

The door-less kitchen has a gas stove with four burners and an oven. There's also a refrigerator and a double sink. Shelves above the sink are used to store dry goods and bottles of pop are stacked in a corner. Perishable foods are in the refrigerator with the bottom row reserved for keeping pop cold. A metal folding chair sits next to the stove; Tressie sits there. Just behind her chair is the back door which locks from the inside. Beyond the door is the alley.

Next to the kitchen is a hallway that leads to the bathroom, which has a commode and a single sink. A bar of soap rests on the sink's tiny vanity. A rack with one hand towel hangs above the sink bowl, right where you would expect a mirror. A black, metal trash can sits underneath the sink and the room is lit by a single, overhead, light bulb. The floor linoleum is checkerboard and two sets of overhead fluorescent lights are constantly buzzing.

The Place has no waitresses. Customers walk up to the counter to place their orders with Algie. A chalkboard mounted on the wall in the dining area lists the available menu items. Customers take a seat on a stool or at one of the tables until their plates are ready for pick up. Every meal is served on a white paper plate; to-go meals are wrapped in aluminum foil. Silver utensils are sorted into large, plastic tumblers at the far end of the counter. When an order is ready, Algie hands the plate (and drink, if ordered) across the counter to the waiting customer, or calls over to a table for guests to come pick up their meal.

Next door to The Place is Clover's Pool Room, Crook's business. "Crook" has a twofold meaning. First, it's short for crooked teeth. Willie's front two molars are turned in opposite directions and four of his bottom teeth are each shifted at a slight angle. Second, the nickname would suit him even without the misaligned teeth because of his reputation for scams, cons, and stinginess.

Although he's Edward's cousin, Algie has never liked him. Her dislike deepened after her husband died and Crook tried to dissuade her from running The Place, offering to handle it for her. She refused. Angered by her rebuff, Crook began a campaign of ugly taunts, which he whispers or mouths to Algie across the lunch counter when he thinks no one is watching or listening.

"You're slow and country."

"You won't last long in the big city on your own without a man."

"You was nothing' in Georgia with Eddie Mack, how you gone be something' now up here without him?"

"Time is on my side. I can wait you out!"

Consistently, Algie turns away from him and gives no reply. Like The Place, Clover's Pool Room has a single front door with two large windows on either side. Nothing is painted on the

14

windows.

Clover's is open every day, except Sunday, so there's no conflict with the storefront church on the other side. Working-class men, many of them from the Westside Cab Company, drop by regularly to talk, lie, and laugh—all in that order.

Clover's has two pool tables and a couple of folding tables and chairs for games dominoes or spades. A little betting is allowed, but the wager is never high enough to cause a fight or worse. There's no poker games played at the tables. Any real gambling takes place out back in the alley with Crook supervising and taking his cut. Pool room regulars often walk over to The Place to eat. Sometimes they walk back to the pool room with their plates, other times they stay and eat in the restaurant. Conversations started at Clover's carry over into The Place and vice versa, so there's a steady stream of comings-and-goings at both establishments.

The Place sees its share of visitors from the storefront church, too. The House of Faith has double doors, but no windows up front. The only natural light comes from two small windows situated high up on either side of the large, open room. Each window opens and closes with a hand crank. The windows are open on Sundays to let in much needed air, and to expel a joyful noise into the ears of any passerby.

The church has a stand-alone heating unit placed against the back wall. Up front, to the left of the makeshift pulpit (a long table anchored by two high-back chairs), the Reverend Alfred Peters has a small chamber (a converted closet). Inside his chamber, there's a card table, two metal folding chairs, and four wooden crates placed side-by-side and filled with various religious books, pamphlets, and loose-leaf notebook paper. There is no window.

A small lamp on the card table provides the only light in the room. In the corner of the chamber, there's a small altar carefully arranged on a white sheet lying on the floor. The altar consists of a gold cross, bible, and four colored candles. The cross is propped up against the closed bible. A small basket is sitting a few inches in front of the cross.

Two candles are placed on each side of the cross/bible display. The green candle is for money, the red candle is for love, the white candle is for health, and the black candle is for power. Each Sunday, before services, Reverend Peters lights the candles, one at-a-time, as he somberly places his written petitions to God inside the basket. After a short prayer, he walks into the main room to begin the service, leaving the unattended candles burning.

To the right of the pulpit, the 10-member choir sits on metal folding chairs. There is no dressing room or bathroom, so choir members either wear their robes to church or put them on before they enter; each choir member purchased or sewed their own robe. The old, upright piano is stationed beneath one of the windows. The only luxury the small congregation has afforded itself are the six, used pew; three on each side of the room. The church's current fund-raising goal is to buy a proper podium and a purple velvet chair for Reverend Peters' holy throne.

The House of Faith does not have a bathroom. If anyone needs to go before the four-hour service is over, they excuse themselves by quietly rising and extending their pointer finger heavenward. They keep their finger firmly extended until they pass through the front doors and outside. They then walk down the sidewalk to use the bathroom at The Place.

Algie has no objection to this bathroom arrangement since many of them will come in and eat in her restaurant after the church service is over.

The storefront church is all activity on Sunday morning beginning at 8:00 AM, but is quiet during the week, except for Wednesday night choir practice. Then, piano chords start and stop while would-be soloists search for notes on limited, short-range vocal chords. It all comes together for Sunday services, but never sounds like the songs they practiced on the previous Wednesday.

The brick building which houses The Place, Clover's, and the House of Faith faces Germantown, the main thoroughfare through Dayton's Westside. Across the street is a similar brick building also with three businesses: Flamingo's, a night club; Tommy Lee's meat market; and Benny's Bar. Further down Germantown, there are row after row of more black-run businesses set-up in shops owned by whites. There's a diner opened only for breakfast, a shoe repair shop, a five-and-dime store, barber/beauty shop, and a record store.

Algie finally pushes herself up from the sofa and, without a word to Chauncey who has fallen back to sleep, heads back to work. As she turns the corner onto Germantown she sees Viola, just walking into The Place. Before Algie can reach the door, she feels the headache already starting — right in the center of her forehead.

TWO

Tressie is in the kitchen stirring a pot of beans when a very agitated Viola swings her body into The Place. With her choir robe swirling around her, she says to no one in particular: "Why do we whoop and holler at funerals like it's the first time it's ever happened? People die every day!"

Sitting on a stool at the counter, Early turns around at the sound coming through the door. "Oh, Lord," he murmurs to himself. He likes sweet Tressie and fun-loving Honey, but he cannot stand to even be in the same room with Viola. "She's a self-righteous, play Christian in high heels and tight dresses," he's said to Algie time-and-time again. "Choir robes don't cover up any sins and everybody knows none of her boyfriends are single mens."

Algie is only a few steps behind Viola and walks in the door as Early is headed out. "Well, babe, I got to go," he says, smiling at Algie before turning to give Viola a disgusted backwards glance.

Viola's eyes flash right back at him and she shouts after him, "Mama's baby! Daddy's maybe?" True, people doubt that Early is Screamie's father. The child bears no resemblance to him or the mother, so there must be a third party involved. However, everyone, except Viola, keeps their suspicions to themselves.

After her unsolicited statement on mourning and death, Viola walks around the counter and pours herself a cup of coffee — no sugar, no cream. Tressie glances over at her sister from the kitchen with neither a frown nor a smile.

Algie asks, "Did a lot of people turn out for the funeral?

"Yes, they had a good crowd," replies Viola, cup in hand, taking a seat on the stool across the counter from her mother. "I was just saying, right before you came in, that all that whooping and hollering was just unnecessary, though. Some people just want to be seen. For goodness sake, Mother Moore was 99 years old! We knew she was going to die."

"Did Mother Moore have any family left to attend her services?"

"She has a son, but he didn't come up. He still lives in Florida somewhere. He's about 80 years old and his kids are up in age, too."

Viola pauses to take a full sip of coffee before continuing. "But those church hens carried on like Mother Moore was a young woman in the prime of life. It was all for show, Mama, and it was embarrassing! I know pastor just about died from the shame of it."

No one in the restaurant offers any comment. Algie and Tressie have heard it all a thousand times before. As for the two lone customers eating at separate tables, they don't know Viola, the church hens, or Mother Moore.

"Anything new going on at Mt. Moriah?" Algie is not really interested, but she doesn't want Viola to drag on about the hens and the funeral.

Viola is fills her cup for the second time and returns to her stool before answering. "Well, the senior choir is getting new robes, so I met with some of the sisters at the church this week to look over the new designs."

"See anything you like?"

Viola pauses a moment to admire her satin, royal blue robe draped over her shoulders and down her back. The cuffs of the robe have double bands of gold along the edges and the wide, V-shaped collar has a large "M" embroidered on the back. "To tell the truth, I like the robes we have now."

Viola April Clover (born on April 27) is two inches taller than her siblings with an embraceable, curved body that could swallow their petite frames. Her skin is always moist as if an internal sprinkler keeps her lightly misted — no matter the temperature. Viola's long, black hair is styled into soft layers that rest on her shoulders like a mink stole. Her eyebrows are drawn into large, high arches that meet her flat, straight bangs. Her face powder is two shades lighter than her skin tone, and several layers of deep red lipstick fill each crevice of her full lips.

Viola often wears the ever present robe like a cape, unzipped and flying revealing a skintight A-line dress underneath. Viola wears spiked-heels with narrow pointed toes that, based on Honey's observation, could "kill a roach in a corner." When introduced to men, Viola looks directly at them as she presses her soft damp hand into their eager palms that she firmly squeezes. She never shakes hands with women.

Algie has tried, unsuccessfully, to get Viola and Honey to again work at The Place. After all, she and Edward had hoped to make this a family business.

"I can't cook," says Viola. "At least that's the opinion around here."

Despite the fact that she's not employed anywhere, Viola has money whenever she needs it.

Honey begged off, too, telling her mother she wanted a job where she could meet some real people.

"Real people come into this restaurant," said Algie.

"Yes, Mama, but they're the folks with the real jobs that come by here to eat," explained Honey. "Like them, I want to be able to buy my own meals and my own fun."

Honey Emerald Clover has eyes like caramel drops. Algie had hoped the light hue in her baby girl's eyes might turn green like Edward's, so she wanted to name her Emerald. Edward wasn't so sure, and besides, he loved those honey, brown eyes just the way they were.

Edward and Algie had six children and she'd hoped that at least one of them would resemble her handsome husband. But the red-yellow beauty of the man she loved must have died on one of the faces of their two stillborn sons. Honey is the most like Edward with a sprinkling of red freckles across the bridge of her nose, which she hides with face powder.

Like her mother and older sister, she is petite but with one notable difference — a fuller and rounder rear end. "No loose ends here," Honey proudly remarks about her shapely behind which she accentuates in pencil-thin skirts and straight-leg, stretch pants. She layers mascara onto her fragile, thin eyelashes until they dart up like sun rays. Her favorite lip color matches her eyes; soft, creamy brown. She shaves her jagged eyebrows and uses a thick brown pencil to redraw them into a smooth arch.

Like Viola, she prefers heels but not the spikes. Her hard, high calves don't need them. Instead, she opts for a shorter heel and a rounder toe, and a lower vamp to reveal her perfectly plumped toe cleavage.

Honey cuts her hair low enough to expose the natural wave. She uses her fingers to frame her face with tiny curls. Algie wishes she would wear it longer but as Honey had threatened, "When I'm old enough I'm cutting my hair. I don't like ponytails and all these cow licks I got from Daddy won't hold any hairstyle".

After Edward's death, the Buick sat in front of the house for an entire year. On her 16th birthday, Honey started the engine and taught herself to drive by guiding the car up-and-down Dunbar Avenue. She's still the only driver in the family. Free-spirited and good-natured, Honey begins partying every Friday evening with her best friend, Ruby, and doesn't stop until Sunday morning. The first to laugh and the last to stop smiling, "Mama, when I die," she declares, "I want you to put on my headstone: 'The world don't owe me a thing, I had a good time!' "

During the week, Honey works at Woodbine's making motor parts for small appliances. Tressie, however, works full-time at The Place and has done so since her father's death. Her husband drops her off on the way to his job in the train yards.

Tressie Julia Clover-Dodd is named for her great-grandmother. She's a mirror image of Algie and has a similar temperament. Tressie wears her brown-black hair in the same ponytail style and has the same kissable pucker. Her husband, Emerson Dodd (everyone calls him by his last name, including Tressie), unloads coal from the train boxcars onto waiting flatbed delivery trucks. Short in stature and modest, Dodd was 30 years old and had never married when he met his future wife at The Place on a Saturday night.

He wasn't a regular. At the invitation of a friend, he had attended a special revival service at the House of Faith and came into the restaurant afterwards for dinner. Six months later, Tressie and Dodd were married by Rev. Peters at the House of Faith and have been members of the church ever since.

After the wedding, Tressie confessed to Algie that she was not in love with Dodd.

"Then why in the world did you marry him?" asked a perplexed Algie. "Nobody was rushing you to get married."

"I didn't want to take the chance that you would change your mind and move back to Georgia. Where would that leave me?"

"You never heard me say I was moving back, not since I made the decision to stay."

"True, but you're always daydreaming about daddy and Dublin. I couldn't take the chance. Besides, what else could I want in a man? Dodd is hardworking, church-going, and does whatever I ask of him."

Tressie's revelation was disappointing for Algie. She wanted her daughters to marry for love, as she had done. That's why she doesn't nag or pressure Viola or Honey about marriage. "Take your time and wait for the right one."

The Place is open for lunch and dinner Tuesday through Sunday. The dinner special is $2.99 for meat, two vegetables, and a slice of cornbread. The meats and vegetables for the dinner special are on a three-day rotation. First, fried chicken alongside string beans with potatoes and macaroni and cheese; next, meat loaf and mashed potatoes topped with mushroom gravy and lima beans on the side; and third, fried pork chops with baked apples and white rice with butter.

In addition to the special, other rotating dinner entrées include salmon patties, neck bones, baked ham (Sundays only), liver and gizzards with white gravy (Screamie's favorite), and pig's feet. The other sides, depending on the space available on the small stove, are fried corn, corn-on-the-cob, cornbread dressing, pinto or navy beans, rutabagas, collard greens, fried cabbage, squash, and steamed spinach with sliced boiled eggs.

Coffee is a nickel with free refills and a bottle of Pepsi or Royal Crown colas are 10 cents. No alcoholic beverages are served. Dessert choices include a slice of cake (yellow with chocolate icing), peach cobbler, chess pie[4], or rice pudding. Algie makes the desserts at home, in the mornings, before The Place opens at noon.

Lunch at The Place is a sandwich on white bread. Choices are a BLT, tuna or chicken salad, or fried fish served with your choice of "hot" fries, coleslaw, or potato salad; dill pickle on the side. The "hot" fries are a big seller at The Place and customers can order them during dinner, too; if it's not too busy. To make "hot" fries, Algie slices medium-size potatoes into thick wedges. She then heats an inch of lard in a cast-iron skillet and fries the potatoes. When the potatoes are nearly done, she adds coarsely chopped pieces of raw onion. Algie prefers Sweet Vidalia onions, but can't find them here; they're only grown in Georgia. When the potatoes are crisp and the onions browned, she scoops them onto a double-stacked paper plate. She adds a sprinkle of salt and a dash of white vinegar, and then uses two forks to coat the fries and onions with a mixture of half ketchup/half hot sauce.

Grandma Julia's fried chicken is another menu favorite. The chicken has to be prepped a day in advance. Algie cuts the birds into four large pieces; wings/breasts and thighs/drumsticks. The chickens' innards, neck, back, and any other assorted pieces are set aside and used for making cornbread dressing or boiled as stock for cooking beans. The cut-up chickens are thoroughly

[4] A custard pie made of eggs, butter, sugar, vanilla, and flour with a cornmeal crust.

cleaned, dried and then placed into a large aluminum bucket. A mixture of eggs, buttermilk, paprika, and crushed garlic is poured over the chicken. Algie puts a clean white dish towel over the mouth of the bucket and places it in the refrigerator overnight.

The next day, she places the cast-iron skillet on the fire and drops several chunks of lard into the pan. While the lard is melting, she drops each chicken half, separately, into a brown paper sack that is half-way filled with white flour seasoned with salt, black pepper, crushed red pepper, and equal pinches of oregano and parsley. Each golden, fried chicken piece is placed on a paper plate all by itself with a paper cup half-filled with honey. The aroma of frying chicken permeates everything in the small restaurant — no escaping it. Some customers even track the rotation of the specials at The Place, so they know when fried chicken will be on the menu again. And, despite repeated customer requests, fried chicken is only available as it comes around in the rotation. "The prep time takes too long," explained Algie. "And, I hate cutting chickens."

Within months of arriving in Dayton, teenaged Viola was involved with the 30-year-old, married cab dispatcher, Harris. It wasn't her first relationship with an older man. There had been others back in Dublin. This time, however, Edward found out and he confronted Harris at his dispatcher's window. He loudly declared Viola and all his daughters off-limits to the cabbies and he backed-up his threat with a large branch he brought with him; banging it several times against the stall causing it to vibrate. Harris got the message and so did the others. But soon after Edward's unexpected death, Viola was again dating cabbies. Now 26 years old (two years younger than Tressie, and two years older than Honey), she's still unmarried and "waiting on the Lord to bring me a good man."

While she waits, Viola continues to spend time with older,

married men including the pastor of her church, Rev. Henry Wilson Farris.

Rev. Farris is a thick, muscular man who uses the power of his masculinity to fully take advantage of every opportunity that presents itself; inside and outside the pulpit.

When he preaches, sweat shines on his coal-black skin like moonlight as he prances across the stage and around the pulpit. He keeps a large, white handkerchief wrapped around his right hand to periodically wipe the pouring sweat from his forehead. His tree-trunk like thighs bulge through his pants, and the muscles in his arms and shoulders roll and push out of his wringing wet jacket (he only wears his pastoral robe for special occasions).

Henry's high-octane voice doesn't need a microphone and he can quote and misquote the Bible from Genesis to Revelation. He's married to Lillian "Pete" Morris–Farris. The marriage is his first, her second. It's also Pete's second time serving as First Lady of a prominent church.

Pete's first husband was Rev. Galen Morris. Galen's father, a minister when he came north from Ocilla, Georgia, was the first ordained pastor of the then-fledgling New Bethel Baptist Church on Euclid Avenue. Pete's parents had come north the same year from Montgomery, Alabama. The two families lived side-by-side in a duplex on West Grand Avenue.

Both Pete and Galen were born in Dayton and grew up together. She is outspoken, ambitious, and controlling. He is soft-spoken, kind, and sensitive. With a Caucasian grandparent on both her maternal and paternal sides, Pete's complexion is starchy, but she can't pass for white. Her broad flat nose, wide, protruding lips, and kinky ash-blonde hair expose her ethnicity. Unlike her younger sister, who got the hair and Anglo features of those white grandparents, Pete looks black and was often reminded by her mother that she must work harder to keep her status.

Pete's parents consented to her marriage to the dark-skinned boy next door since his family had a standing in the community, and a steady cash flow from New Bethel's coffers.

By the time they married, one month after high school graduation, Galen was already an associate pastor at New Bethel along with two other young ministers. However, unlike the other two associates, Galen's sermons were lackluster and his relationship with the church body was almost nonexistent. His father openly worried that his own son might not be his successor.

Pete and Galen had been married three years, when the elder Morris was killed in a car accident. She quickly moved to secure the pulpit for her husband. Pete threatened to expose one of the associate ministers, who had fathered an out-of-wedlock child with a young choir member. The other minister agreed to step aside for a one-time cash payment. Without the burden of his father's scrutiny, Galen's sermons improved and Pete continued her father-in-law's campaign to "grow the church".

Ten years later, the childless couple had successfully increased New Bethel's membership rolls to more than 800. Rev. Galen Morris was now beloved, but First Lady Pete Morris was feared.

Pete met Henry when "the young minister everybody in Dayton is talking about" was invited to speak at New Bethel. Henry's sermon had left Pete breathless, along with the other women who filled the first three rows to get a look at the new, single minister. A year later, Galen stepped down from the pulpit; Pete called it a heart condition, his doctors' diagnosed a nervous breakdown. A power struggle at New Bethel ensued and it ended with Pete marginalized in the new church hierarchy. Dethroned, she sought refuge at Mt. Moriah.

When Pete first arrived there, many in the congregation welcomed her. They'd heard what happened over at New Bethel and, since their preacher wasn't married, Mt. Moriah needed a matriarch.

Pete gratefully stepped into the role and, initially, executed her duties with humility and respect towards all. Eventually, she and Henry began having dinner meetings at her house to discuss church affairs with Galen silently sitting nearby. One evening, after a meal of smothered chicken with candied yams, turnip greens, and cornbread, Pete sat down on the couch opposite Henry. Galen had gone to bed.

"Henry, I know plenty of folks at New Bethel who are dissatisfied with the way things are being handled over there."

"That may be Sister Morris, but what can we do about it?"

"Let's hold a revival! We'll call it an 'Old Time Religion' meeting. We'll talk it up among the members and the word will spread. Tell them we're bringing back the religion we all knew down South. Two spirit-filled days, spirit-filled days of down-home prayer, songs, and blessings."

Henry listened and chose his words carefully. "That's a great idea," he began slowly. "Many people still miss their home church from down South. But, I'm surprised you thought of that Sister Morris."

Henry saw her hurt and defensive frown and quickly explained. "What I mean is, you told me you were born right here in Dayton. So, you did not grow up in the South like many of us did."

Pete smiled and stared into the eyes of the sexiest man she's ever known. "That's true Henry. But I know what folks want. Oftentimes what they need, long before they even know it themselves."

The next day, Pete moved Galen into her parents' home.
The dinner meetings with Henry now last throughout the night.
Pete and her clique of women (called "hens" by Viola and others
in the church who are opposed to their influence) are running Mt.
Moriah's usher board, women's missionary, choirs, Sunday
school, and nearly every other church committee; except the
deacon's board.

Pete's hens include Hazel Fuqua. A widow, Hazel's emaciated
physique is perfectly paired with her equally thin-skinned
personality. Easily offended and chronically paranoid, she debuts
a new wig every Sunday, but still wears her wedding band, 20
years after her husband's death. Hazel speaks of him as if he were
still alive and offers her dead husband's opinions from the grave.

Deborah James is considered the prettiest of the hens. She's petite,
shapely and wears an array of tailored suits with ruffled white
blouses. Deborah's matching hats often have a short veil that casts
a shadow across her clear, gray eyes. She recently remarried for
the third time saying, "I'm going to keep doing it until I get it
right!"

Charlotte Milton is the youngest hen. Her face is decorated with
the latest brand of thick, blue eye shadow; heavy, black eyeliner;
and candy red lipstick. She's from Jackson, Mississippi, and
travels home every summer to visit her mother. Charlotte is 30
years old, single, and looking. Finding a husband is her number
one priority and she won't rest until "the Lord answers my
prayer."

Margaret "Peggy" Linwood and her husband, Boss, have seven
children. Boss is the senior deacon in the church and Henry's
confidante. It was Boss that encouraged his pastor to marry Pete,
telling the younger man, "None of these young, hot sisters can

bring you the respect or power that she can."

Rounding out the flock is Geneva Black. She attends most church services alone because her truck driver husband is often away on the road. Their six children are all grown, but none of them is "saved." Geneva helps with the planning, but doesn't participate in many of the church's special activities. The numerous duties she's obligated to perform for her large — mostly unemployed — family keeps her busy all the time.

Despite their dominance, Pete and the hens are constantly challenged by two sisters that Viola calls the bulls — Norma Jean and Gloria Collins.

Norma Jean and Gloria are 38 and 39 years old, respectively. They are co-owners of an unnamed beauty shop they run from the basement of the home they share. The shop has afforded them a comfortable means of living and their generous monetary contributions to Mt. Moriah have given them a voice in the church.

Norma Jean met Henry first. He came by the shop to pick up his girlfriend, who remains one of Norma Jean's best clients. The sisters eagerly began attending Henry's Sunday services that were being held in the Masonic Lodge on Germantown Street. They supported Henry financially, domestically (they washed and cleaned his clothes), and sexually.

It was the Collins sisters who put up the cash to buy the two-story, brick and wood American foursquare house that became Mt. Moriah Baptist Church. Each year, since the purchase, a new renovation or addition has been added to keep pace with the rapid growth of the congregation. The 1,200-seat church is now the second largest black church in Dayton; second only to New Bethel.

Henry baited Norma Jean and Gloria with promises of marriage, which he tossed between the two sisters. Before meeting Henry, Norma Jean and Gloria had never had a serious disagreement about anything. After meeting him, the rivalry kept them in a state of war. Norma Jean and Gloria closely resemble each other; some people assume they're twins. Both have round, unshapely figures, excessive hair growth (they shave daily), and broad shoulders.

Additionally, Gloria must also contend with a heavy, raspy voice that is two octaves lower than her sister's. However, both sisters are proficient singers whose voices add emotion and depth to the choir at Mt. Moriah. The sisters compensate for their extra testosterone by wearing bright, bold, colored outfits with matching hats, purses, and shoes. They smother their bodies with baby powder, followed by a generous dousing of Evening in Paris cologne.

One Sunday, without a word to either one of them, Henry stood up in the pulpit and announced his engagement to Pete. Norma Jean and Gloria were devastated. Even some members of Mt. Moriah had expected that Henry would choose one of the sisters to marry, if not for their looks, certainly for the money. During the first year of Pete and Henry's marriage, the sisters kept a low profile, not participating in any church events, except for the choir. They began coming late for services and would leave early before the final prayer.

And then, the following Easter, with the soft piano keys of a familiar song playing in the background, Henry symbolically opened the doors of the church. Standing in front of the pulpit, he extended his right hand towards the overflow crowd and in a slow, melodious cadence said:

> *Let the doors of the church be open, Come in,*
> *Help us to build Mt. Moriah,*

On a true and solid foundation, a foundation,
That won't give away.

He repeated the invitation in the same manner several times, allowing newcomers enough time to work up their nerve to walk to the front of the church. And then Henry saw her.

Viola approached the pulpit with her head reverentially bowed toward the ground. Her navy blue, A-line sheath dress was snug as a glove and stopped at the top of her knees. A white ruffle trim was sewn around the hemline, at the end of each sleeve, and along a plunging neckline. Her matching hat resembled a pirate's brim and a white crinoline scarf was tied around the hat's band with the excess flowing across the back of her shoulders.

When Viola reached the pulpit, she raised her head and returned Henry's gaze. He stopped talking. In a passionate, steady voice, she testified before the church and God that what she heard and saw in Henry was the salvation that she had been seeking.

The hens immediately begin flapping; adjusting their hats, exchanging glances, loudly clearing their throats, and turning around in their seats. The bulls, however, sat up straight and spontaneously emerged from their depressed stupor. Sister Viola Clover was the answer to their prayers — revenge.

Viola and Henry were lovers before the next Sunday service. Norma Jean and Gloria quickly made her an integral part of the choir, even though the Viola can barely sing on key. Viola accepted their friendship because she needed allies in the church. Besides, being around Norma Jean and Gloria was more like being around men anyway, since they are so thick and hairy.

The Collins sisters do Viola's hair for free, provide her with transportation, and their guest room is reserved exclusively for her use. The rivalry between the wife and the mistress has split the church, but reunited Norma Jean and Gloria in sisterly love.

Viola finishes her third cup of coffee and announces she's walking home to take a nap. Neither Tressie nor Algie acknowledge her departure; they are too busy getting ready for the dinner crowd. However, Algie pauses to glance at the clock and begins a silent countdown in her head.

Chauncey is asleep in her chair when Viola enters the house. She awakens just as Viola is passes her, headed for the bedroom. "That you, Vi?" asks Chauncey, keeping her opened eyes downcast.

Viola doesn't answer. She despises the old woman who is "always talking against me with her eyes".

"Did you hear me girl?"

There is no sound from the bedroom.

Chauncey pinches off a fresh piece of snuff and rises from her chair. She begins chewing slowly at first and then picks up the pace as she walks angrily into the communal bedroom.

"I said do you hear me girl?" Chauncey spits snuff into the room as she stands in the doorway, her head brushing the top of the door's frame. Viola steps out of her heels and rolls her eyes before turning her back on her grandmother.

"You think you too good to speak to me? Who do you think you are girl! I wiped your nasty behind and filled your crying mouth with milk even after I knew you were full. You don't have any right to disrespect me, especially with the life you're leading. And nobody's forgetting the sacrifices that have been made on that very bed you're standing over!"

The phone rings. Viola twists her angry body pass Chauncey and into the living room. "Hello?"

"Viola April Clover, hand the phone to Mama and go back into the bedroom. Close the door behind you," orders Algie.

"Mom, I didn't start it!"

"Stop! Just do as I say."

Viola extends the phone towards Chauncey, who reluctantly takes it. She knows who it is.

"Ain't nothing for you to say to me Algie. I'm going to my chair to listen to the radio." Chauncey hangs up the phone and sits back down.

Viola and Chauncey alone in a room — any room — is a volatile situation. Algie knew the two would be at each other as soon as Viola stepped through the door, but she couldn't leave the restaurant and Tressie shorthanded during dinnertime. The phone was the next best thing.

THREE

Tressie and Dodd have been trying to have baby since they married. Tressie's first pregnancy ended in a miscarriage. The second one went the full nine months, but the baby boy only lived six hours. The failed pregnancies have drawn Tressie and Dodd closer, but inflamed the cold war between Tressie and Viola. Because for every one of Tressie's blessed angels that should have lived, Viola has had her healthy, growing babies "cut, bagged, and tossed". Tressie cannot openly discuss her sister's abortions because Algie has mandated that no one discuss Viola's sicknesses. Rather, it's Dodd who hears her anguished complaints to God.

"On a regular basis, Viola breaks at least half of the 10 commandments. She murders her innocent babies. She steals other women's husbands. She lies to cover up her nasty adultery. She covets every man that is not her own. And, some of these sins she has committed on the Sabbath!

"Dodd, you and I don't do any of those things," Tressie wails. "We faithfully attend church services. We pray every day. Yet, we can't keep a child alive in this world. And I just found out that fat rabbit might be pregnant again!"

Like a flash flood, Tressie's tears plummet from her eyes. She almost drops the pan of cornbread she is sliding out of the oven. Dodd quickly steps over to help. He embraces his wife and she leans hard against his chest, drying her eyes on his undershirt.

Dodd feels the same pain and is equally disgusted with Viola's disregard for life. He has a daughter from a previous relationship, but lost track of her years ago. He doesn't know what Tressie's sins are, but perhaps God doesn't trust him with another child. Unbeknownst to Tressie, he's approached Viola privately and begged her to carry at least one baby to full-term, promising that he and Tressie would gladly take the baby and raise it as their own. "This way, you can accept your inheritance from God. Just like the bible says and have your sins washed clean." Viola never looked at Dodd. She walked away from him, wrapping her choir robe tighter and tighter around her body like a tourniquet.

Tressie and Dodd live in an apartment about eight blocks from The Place. Tressie sits in a white, rocking chair strategically placed in the corner of the living room. A metal TV tray is next to the rocker. On the tray there's an empty glass, her oversized bible, a book of crossword puzzles, and a yellowing, dog-eared *The Watchtower* magazine.

Tressie got the magazine from Miss Stewart, the Jehovah's Witness lady that periodically stops by The Place. Algie lets Miss Stewart read a scripture and leave her magazines on the counter. Tressie would scan the magazines, reading the titles and the captions under the pictures. But one day an article caught her eye and she's held onto that particular magazine since; the one she keeps here on her table at home. The April 15, 1954, issue of *The Watchtower* had a question from a reader that asked: "Will a baby that dies shortly after birth have a resurrection if its' parents are faithful servants of Jehovah?"

It had never occurred to Tressie that her babies could live again.

She always thought that God just took babies to heaven to become angels.

She underlined the response: "Although a child dying a few hours or days or even a year after birth may not have developed a life pattern or intelligent memory … if time had been allowed for these to develop they would have resulted in a definite personality … Jehovah God and Christ Jesus are able to note and reproduce all these latent tendencies in a babe and to reproduce them in the resurrection …"

Resurrection. The mere thought of it takes the edge off Tressie's sadness. She repeatedly reads the question and the answer. Algie and Dodd have expressed concern that she gives to much weight to the magazine's response. Dodd told her, "Dead babies are angels living with God. They don't need mothers anymore." But Tressie holds onto the magazine. "I read the bible, too and I accept God at his word."

After Dodd drops Tressie off, within seconds Early comes into the still closed restaurant and hands Screamie over to her. However, he doesn't immediately go to the poolroom; he waits for Algie. She comes 15 minutes later, carrying today's desserts. Early tells her that he needs a little money and she takes some cash from the register. Algie playfully pinches Screamie's cheek and tells Tressie she must return home for the peach cobbler and will take the toddler with her. Early is already next door.

Tressie is in the kitchen when she again hears the door open. It's Rev. Peters. She welcomes him with a cheerful, "Hello, pastor. What can I get you?"

"Just a piece of cake and a cup of coffee; I've been working on my sermon for tomorrow and needed to take a break."

Tressie walks over to the counter and removes the aluminum foil from the cake Algie just brought in. "How big a slice do you want?"

"Be generous."

She slices the cake and places it on a paper plate and sets a fork on the counter next to it. She pours him a cup of coffee and takes her mother's seat on the stool behind the counter.

"How's your family?" he asks, as he begins to consume the cake. "I mean your mother and your sisters."

"They're all doing just fine. I appreciate you asking about them."

"How's Honey doing?"

Honey? Tressie is surprised. "She's doing just fine. Why are you asking about her pastor?" The question tumbles out of her mouth before she can catch herself.

Rev. Peter continues eating his cake and does not look up. He takes long sip of coffee before replying, "just asking, no reason."

Tressie rests her hands on the counter. She wants to burst out laughing, but manages to control herself and instead says, "Well, I'll say." Does her pastor have an interest in Honey?

Despite the affection she and Dodd have for their minister, there's no way she would let him get involved with any woman in her family. Everybody knows Rev. Peters has a white liver. His first wife died in childbirth. The second one, at 31 years of age, was dead of natural causes. And the third wife was hit and killed by a car. Plus, he's too old for her baby sister and definitely not Honey's type. Honey is a Christian, but not a Sunday churchgoer. And, she won't be giving up the party life anytime soon.

Tressie expresses none of this to Rev. Peters. She doesn't want to hurt his feelings, especially since there's no need. He won't get past "hello" with Honey.

Tressie returns to the kitchen, leaving Rev. Peters alone to finish his cake and coffee. She hears the coins drop on the counter and calls out a "good-bye" to him.

As he walks down the sidewalk back to his church, Rev. Peters talks softly to himself. It's a practice he learned as a boy; from your lips to God's ear. That's what makes things happen. Now, he'll just wait for his chance to woo that pretty little Clover girl.

At the house, Algie is sitting on the sofa with Screamie asleep across her lap. The child was barely awake when Early dropped her off. Since The Place is not busy, she decides to let Screamie sleep for a few minutes before carrying her back to the restaurant. She's also concerned that Chauncey has been unusually quiet since they came in the door and she wasn't that way when she left her earlier.

"Everything all right, Mama?"

Chauncey doesn't reply or move in her seat.

Algie looks over at her mother with a half-smile and waits a few seconds before asking again. "Mama, I know you heard me. What's wrong with you?"

Chauncey remains silent and motionless.

In a flat voice, devoid of emotion, Algie answers Chauncey's silence. "Well, I guess you're having a heart attack. Let me know when to call the ambulance for you."

Algie lays her head back into the sofa's cushions and, like

Screamie, closes her eyes to grab a quick nap. She didn't sleep well last night and woke up tired. Just as she feels that sweet roll of slumber overtaking her body, she's startled by a hard slap on her hand.

Algie sits up in her seat and instinctively embraces Screamie to keep the sleeping child from falling to the floor. Chauncey is standing over her, both hands on her hips, with a twisted scowl on her face. "Don't act like you don't hear me Algie. Them papers are sitting over there on that chest!"

Although she's only slept a few minutes, Algie is groggy. "What are you talking about Mama? I was asleep. You wouldn't talk to me when I was awake. Why did you wait until I closed my eyes?"

Chauncey walks over and snatches the envelope from the lowboy. "This just came in the mail." She thrusts it towards Algie who takes the envelope but doesn't open it. Algie moves slowly, allowing herself more time to get fully awake. The return address on the envelope is Dublin, Georgia. As she opens the letter, the flap releases easily and Algie knows that's because Chauncey has already opened it.

Algie unfolds a single sheet of paper that is addressed to her. It's from Mr. Snell. Snell is the owner of the land and the house where they used to live. He writes that he's heard about Eddie Mack's death, the hardships she's faced as a widow, and how she has longed to return home. He tells her to come back and he'll work out good terms for work and wages for her and her daughters.

Algie is stunned. How in the world would Mr. Snell know how to reach her, let alone what is happening to them in Dayton? They were not on friendly terms with this white man and have had no contact with him since they left. And, what's this about her "longing to return home?" Algie puts the letter in her lap and

40

stares at the return address. She tries to figure out what this could mean. It takes only a few minutes for one name to come to mind — Crook!

"What you going to do about it? I say we take him up on his offer and go back to where we belong."

Algie carefully picks up the sleeping child and positions Screamie over her shoulder. As she stands, she tosses the letter onto the couch. "Mama, I didn't write to Mr. Snell but I know who did. As for his offer, we won't be accepting it."

"Why not? What have you got here that you can't have back at home?"

As she opens the door to leave, Algie turns to face her mother. "I prayed all night about deciding to stay in Dayton or to return to Dublin. As I lay on my pillow that night, part of my thinking included this fact. Slavery ended in 1865. Eight years from now, it will be 1965. That's 100 years. Most people live 70 or 80 years. You're 78 years old yourself! Think of it, we're only one generation away from the plantation. If you really want to go back, I will help you. But as for me and my girls, we're not turning back!" Algie didn't wait for a response.

She walks back to The Place, barely noticing her surroundings. Anger is pulsating through her body and throbbing at the tips of her fingers and toes. Crook is going to find his way out-of-her-business and she's going to help him. Action speaks louder than words and Algie knows exactly what to do.

Early is sitting on a stool at the counter when she returns. He's come to take Screamie home. 'So, soon?" asks Algie, as she kisses the sleeping child on her forehead and hands her over.

"Thanks, babe. I'll bring her back tomorrow." He heads outside to a waiting pick-up truck, leaving Algie with no explanation for the sudden departure.

"Why did he bother to bring her today, if she couldn't stay?" asks Tressie.

"I don't know. I guess he thinks he's doing his duty by picking her up every weekend."

Tressie shrugs. "The grease is hot; you can fry the chicken now." She nods towards the door as a very tall, young man is coming in.

"May I help you?" asks Algie.

"Yes, ma'am, I'm looking for Mrs. Algie Clover."

Algie raises her eyebrows slightly in surprise. "That's me. How can I help you?"

"I'm Nathan Farmer and I'd like to talk to you, if you have a few minutes?"

"Is this about the restaurant Mr. Farmer or are you trying to sell me something?"

Nathan lets out a nervous laugh. "No, ma'am. I'm not a salesman. Actually, I want to speak to you about your daughter Viola."

Again, Algie raises her eyebrows with a puzzled look. Tressie grunts and goes back to the kitchen.

"Have a seat Mr. Farmer. What about Viola?"

"Well Mrs. Clover, to begin, I know Viola very well. We've been dating for some time. I met her at Mt. Moriah. Since she told me that her father had died, I thought it best to approach you, her mother."

Algie says nothing and her unblinking stare isn't helping. Nathan is already nervous. He begins to perspire and clutches his hands in a way not normal for him.

"You see, ma'am, I've heard, not from Viola yet, that she's with child. I'm sure it's mine. So, I want to do the right thing and get married. But before I propose, I wanted her father's, or in this case, her mother's consent." Sweat is now pouring from the top of Nathan's head. The three-piece now feels like a diver's wet suit; snug and clingy.

Algie takes her time and she doesn't divert her gaze. "Where are you from, Mr. Farmer?"

"Oh, uh, yes, ma'am. I'm from St. Louis. My father moved us here about 10 years ago. I've got five brothers. My mother died before we came here. We're a Christian family, Mrs. Clover and my daddy taught us boys to take responsibility for our actions. I do love Viola, so this isn't just a duty for me, if that's what you're thinking." Nathan pauses to catch his breath.

Algie pauses, too. She didn't know Viola was pregnant again and she seriously doubts that Nathan is the father.

"I appreciate your honesty, Mr. Farmer. And I want you to know that I would have no objections to any of my daughters marrying a fine, Christian man like you. However, you really need to first discuss this with Viola. If she hasn't told you that she's pregnant, you can't be really sure it's true."

"You mean Mrs. Clover, she hasn't told you, her own mother, that she's pregnant?"

"No, Mr. Farmer, she hasn't mentioned it."

Confused, Nathan finally says, "Well, thank you ma'am for speaking with me. I'll take your advice and do just as you say. Thanks for taking time to speak with me." Nathan stands up so fast, he's dizzy. He stumbles towards the door and makes a quick exit.

Algie continues to sit for a few minutes as Viola's third pregnancy settles inside her now throbbing head. She knows what's coming next. Viola walks around the house in her nightgown all-day long, never leaving the house. Just before dark, there will be a knock at the door. It will be the witch, dressed in layers of two — two long-sleeved, ankle-length dresses; two white cardigans; two pairs of white socks; two earrings in a single, pierced hole. She'll wear black, canvas flat shoes and a poorly knitted, white floppy hat. Her shoulder-length hair will be a tangled mess of white, gray, black, and yellow strands of varying lengths. Every feature on her face droops; eyes, lips, jaws, and even her double chin.

The witch walks everywhere and only stops at a house if she's been called there. Slung over her shoulders is a black, knitted handbag with the tools of her trade: alcohol; mineral oil; camphor; Kotex pads; and knitting needles. She carries a gallon bottle of bleach in her right hand, leaving her left arm free to swing wildly as she walks.

The first time she came to the house, it was winter with a couple of inches of snow on the ground. Algie didn't know that Viola was pregnant. She had slammed the door and screamed "get off my porch"! The witch said nothing, but waited. Viola tapped her mother on the shoulder and motioned for Algie to move to the side. Instead, Algie opened the door and walked past the witch into the cold outside, leaving her coat behind. She walked all the way to The Place, went inside, and sat there in the dark.

Afterwards, Viola was sick in bed with fever for a week. She took so many aspirins her ears were ringing. Honey helped Algie change the bed sheets and pour cool water into Viola. Algie walked home from The Place every half-hour to check on Viola. More than once, she paused on her way back from the house to vomit out the disgust, anger, and pain that kept her nauseated for weeks after Viola's abortion. Chauncey refused, in her words, to "help clean up after the murder."

The second one was no easier. In fact, it was worse, because Algie decided to stay. Leaning against the wall behind the witch, the smell of exposed flesh and blood filled Algie's nostrils, making breathing difficult. She kept pinching her nose both to block and release the deadly odor. Viola lay on the bed, pillows propping up each bent knee with her legs parted wide open. A large piece of heavy plastic is underneath her body.

The witch went about her work of tearing and peeling back the resistant mass of tissue, mucous, and life without hesitation, comment, or emotion. Her knitting needles clicking back-and-forth through the birth canal until a heaping, smoldering mass was expelled onto the newspapers stacked on the floor at the foot of the bed for that purpose. A torrent of blackish blood followed. The witch used alcohol, mineral oil, and camphor soaked rags to dam the flow of blood. The only sound in the room came from Viola's muffled moans and choking sobs. All the while, the top of Algie's head felt like a block of ice, but her feet felt as if she were standing on hot coals.

Algie continued to watch in agony as the witch bagged up the remnants of her now dead grandchild and tossed him/her to the side. The witch finished by dipping more rags, barehanded, into a bucket of bleach to wipe down the splatter on the bed's frame and the floor. Her work completed, she repacked her bag and left behind a stack of sanitary napkins at the foot of the bed.

That time it took Viola longer to recover. And, Algie's nausea left her so fatigued and dehydrated that during one trip back from the house, she fainted right at the front door of The Place. A man coming out of Crook's saw her fall and rushed over to help. When she recovers, a crying Tressie was kneeling down beside her. Benny was leaning over Tressie and one of his bar waitresses was pressing a cold towel to her head.

"Mama, are you going to come and fry this chicken or what? It's getting late!" Algie gets up, back in the present and back to work.

Honey parks the car in front of The Place. She and Ruby want a bite to eat, but first go into the pool room; the latter has spotted a male friend through the window. As they enter, the two young women are greeted with a chorus of whistles and pick-up lines, which they acknowledge only with smiles. Ruby walks over to her friend's table and is soon leaning against him with her arm draped across his shoulder. Honey sees Early sitting at a table playing dominoes as she goes to the bar in the back to greet her Uncle Crook. Crook is talking to an attractive man that she's never seen before. Both men smile at the sight of her.

"Hey my honey child, how's my favorite niece? What are you and Ruby up to this fine Friday evening?"

Honey leans across the bar to embrace Crook. "The same old stuff. But, I'm a little hungry. I missed lunch at work today, so I want to get a plate of food from Mom before we hit the streets." The man standing at the bar with her uncle is still smiling at her.

Bodacious "Bo" Johnson has a permanent summer tan that complements his neat, black mustache and perfectly cropped hair. His hypnotic smile ends on each cheek into deep dimples and, if he were a woman, many would assume his luscious eyelashes were fakes.

"Who's your friend?" Honey asks her uncle.

"This is Bo. Bo, meet my niece, Honey."

Honey and Bo exchange "hellos" and begin a conversation of small talk. Someone at the dominoes table signals for Crook and he leaves the couple alone at the bar.

"Would you like to go out with me and my friend Ruby tonight?
"Where you headed?"

"Here and there, wherever the night may take us."

Bo stands up straighter. "OK, Miss Honey. You lead the way."

"Ruby and I are going next door first to eat." Then, Honey adds proudly, "The Place is my mother's restaurant." She gives Ruby the signal that it's time to go, and Ruby and her friend join them.

The Place is crowded. Ten people are standing in line and all four tables are taken. Honey leads her entourage to the far end of the counter and tells them, "I'll get us some food, but first let me help Mom and Tressie." She walks to the front of the line and asks the waiting couple what they would like to order. Algie and Tressie see Honey and they simultaneously nod a thank you.

When the line has dwindled to only two customers, Honey fills four plates with food and carries them over to her waiting friends. They eat standing up and talk about a couple of night spots they should visit. A table finally becomes available, just as they're finishing their meals, and the foursome sit down. Honey takes away their empty plates and soon returns with thick slices of chess pie.

"Coffee or pop?" she asks. Ruby and her friend want Pepsi, but Bo asks for coffee.

The two couples are enjoying their dessert and conversation;

47

oblivious to a woman that has just entered The Place and paused at the entrance.

Algie is clearing off tables and bringing out new orders, but she notices her. After setting a plate down in front of a customer, she walks towards the woman and asks if she would like to place an order? The woman shakes her head "no". The night air is temperate, but she's wearing a heavy, wool coat and gloves. Her hair is unkempt and she keeps blinking her eyes. Algie tries again. "Are you looking for somebody?" Again, the woman shakes her head. Algie shrugs and returns to her work.

Honey, who is sitting with her back to the door, is not aware of the woman's presence. Then, without warning, the woman lunges toward Honey. She jumps back just as quickly and runs out the door. Bo looks up at the woman and Honey turns around slightly in her chair.

"What was that all about?" Honey raises her eyebrows and rolls her eyes. The group has finished eating and she gets up to clear away their plates.

"Ouch!"

Ruby asks, "What's wrong Honey? Too much pie?"

"No, I just felt a funny pinch in my back." Honey reaches her arm around to rub the sore spot on her back. When she brings her hand back, Bo jumps, knocking his chair over.

"Blood!" Honey, you're bleeding!"

Everyone in the restaurant turns towards the noise. Ruby begins screaming as Honey sinks to her knees. A pool of blood is creating a sickening pattern across the back of Honey's pink wool sweater. Bo drops to the floor alongside her, but is afraid to touch the wound for fear he'll make the pain worse.

Algie and Tressie run to Honey's side and along with Bo form a protective circle around her. Algie instructs Tressie to get up and "call for an ambulance!"

Honey remains on her hands and knees; her head hanging limply. She is not crying and doesn't say a word. Bo uses one hand to caress her downcast face, and with the other hand pats Algie on the back. "Everything is going to be fine," he reassures them both. "I'm going next door to get Crook. I'll be right back."

As Bo leaves, Algie sends Tressie to the kitchen for towels. Several patrons, meanwhile, have quietly slipped out of The Place, leaving behind their half-eaten meals.

"Does it hurt Honey?" asks Algie, as she layers towels over the wound; pressing them down to compress the gaping hole.

Her back hurts, but Honey manages to tell her mother that the pain is not "too bad". She doesn't feel faint but asks to lie down. Algie and Tressie roll Honey onto her side and lay her down on the floor.

"Don't worry," says Algie with a quivering smile. "Remember, you've got Clover blood in you. It's thicker than water and stronger than bootleg wine."

Honey chuckles softly and tells her mother she'll be alright.

Bo returns with Crook. When they open the door to The Place, the wail of the siren fills the room. Crook had asked Early to come with them, but he remained next door.

Algie climbs into the ambulance with Honey. Tressie finds the keys to the car in Honey's purse and hands them to Bo, who follows in the Buick with Crook, Tressie, and Ruby riding with him.

The knife wound is not serious. "Likely, a small, paring knife," observes the doctor. "It wasn't put in deep enough to puncture any major organs. "

The police ask them all a barrage of questions about the unidentified woman, but no one knows her. Honey only moans and never replies to the officers' inquiries.

Six hours later, she is back at home in bed; her mother on one side and Crook on the other. Bo is sitting on the couch, watched by a visibly shaken Chauncey. Dodd and Tressie are there, too, sitting next to Bo. Dodd had met them at the hospital and transported Algie and Honey back home in his car. He dropped Ruby off at her apartment on the way back. Viola's whereabouts are unknown.

Crook squeezes Honey's hand and asks, "Did you recognize the woman?" Honey says nothing and wipes tears from her eyes with her free hand.

"Crook this can wait until the morning," says Algie. "She needs some rest." Crook agrees and leaves the bedroom. "I'll be around to check on you later today."

As Algie slips the nightgown over her head, Honey, fighting fatigue and drowsiness, asks her mother to "stop for a minute."

"Sorry baby, I didn't mean to hurt you."

"You didn't, Mama. I just need to say something before I pass out; just in case I don't wake up."

"You'll wake up. "I'll see to that!"

"No, Mom. I need to tell you something now. I know who that woman was."

Algie gets the gown on and helps Honey lie back into a stack of pillows.

"What do you mean you know her. Why didn't you tell the police? Why did she stab you? Algie can barely catch a breath between her questions.

"I don't know her name. But I know her husband. And that's why I think she stabbed me. I'm not mad at her. I might have done the same thing."

Algie places her daughter's hands inside of her own. "That's not like you Honey. You don't mess with other women's husbands."

"No, I don't. But, I didn't know he was married until after we had dated awhile. I broke up with him, but the word is, his wife was still out to get me because he left her anyway. I don't know where he is. But she blames me."

"Do you know how to find her?

"No and I won't look for her."

Algie squeezes Honey's hands and then gently releases them. "Get some sleep, you'll feel better in the morning."

Algie closes the French doors behind her as she walks into the living room full of anxious faces. "Honey's fine. Just tired and sleepy from all the drugs they gave her. Go on home. I'll let you know if anything changes."

Tressie kisses her mother goodnight and follows Dodd out the door. Algie thanks Bo for all his help. He asks if she has a piece of paper so he can write his phone number down for her. She finds paper and pen in the top drawer of the lowboy. Once everyone is gone and Chauncey has gone back to bed, Algie sits, still fully clothed, on the sofa. She leans back and closes her eyes, but the phone starts ringing.

"Algie? Miss Algie?" The caller keeps repeating her name.

"Yes. Who is this? What do you want?"

"It's me, Benny. Sorry to call you so late at your home, but I just heard about Honey. Is she OK?"

Algie breathes a sigh of relief. "Yes, Benny. She's going to be fine. Sorry, I sounded so rude. It's been a long night and I've never heard your voice on the phone before."

"Oh, right, right," laughs Benny. "I hope you don't mind me calling."

"No, not at all. I appreciate your concern."

"Is there anything I can do? Do you need anything?"

"No. The only thing I need right now Benny is some rest."

"I understand. Just let me know if you need anything. Goodnight, Algie."

FOUR

Champ is Miss Adele's bulldog. She and her dog live next door to Algie on Dunbar. Champ is blind in one eye and his left hind leg is deformed into a short, twisted knot; dangling from his side. The dog often hobbles up and down the street, stopping to sniff a trash can or something on the ground. Champ is not vicious and has never bitten anyone.

As Algie turns the corner onto her street, she stops. Champ is standing in the middle of Dunbar with a football helmet on his head.

"What in the world?" Algie wonders aloud to herself.

She cautiously continues down the street and is startled when the door to her own house is suddenly flung open. Chauncey is standing at the top of the stairs with a broom under her arm.

"Stay back girl! Everybody who touches this dog is gonna die. Everybody who looks at him is gonna get symptoms!"

Stunned, Algie obeys and stands still. Her mother is poised for battle and Champ is still standing in the middle of the street.

"What's wrong with him? Who put that helmet on Champ's head?

Chauncey adjusts the broom handle under her arm and points it like a rifle. Champ looks over at her and then lies down in the middle of the street.

"Mama! I said what in the world is going on here?"

Algie begins slowly walking down the street again. Champ looks silly, but just as benign as he's always been. He's not barking or making any threatening moves towards her or her mother. All the same, Algie keeps some space between herself and the dog, just in case.

"Careful! He's a mad dog!"

Champ drops his head on his front paws, causing the helmet to tilt slightly above his head.

"Where is Miss Adele?"

Frustrated, Algie stops and puts her hands on her hips. "Mama, I said, where is Miss Adele?"

Algie decides it's time to rescue Champ from a predicament she's now sure her mother has caused. She begins whistling at Champ to get his attention. He sits up on his hind legs and the helmet tilts forward over his eyes.

"Come here boy. Come on. It's OK." Algie speaks consolingly to the dog.

"I told you he's a mad dog! Get back before you get bit!

Chauncey takes one step down the stairs and grasps the broom handle with both hands, the bristles aimed toward Champ.

"Mama! For the last time, what have you done to this poor dog? And why have you done it?"

"He's got rabies! That's why I got Eddie Mack's old helmet and slammed it on his head to keep him from biting somebody."

The helmet had belonged to Edward, even though he'd never played football. The men in Dublin played softball, but one evening he came home with it. Algie can't remember how or why he brought it. Edward placed the helmet on their front porch and there it remained, until he tossed it in the car, the day they began the trip north.

"How did you get the helmet on his head?"

"I snuck up behind him and I slapped him across the behind with this broom and he fell over. Then, I straddled him and rammed the helmet on his head.

Poor, poor dog, thought Algie. This crazy woman has got nothing better to do than terrorize an old dog.

"Mama, why do you think he's got rabies?"

Chauncey flips the broom to her other arm and points the handle towards Champ's rear end. "Look at his backside! The fur is completely eaten up with it!"

Algie is no longer apprehensive or afraid. She quickly walks over to Champ and leans over to look at the dog's behind. It was true, he has huge bald spots. And what little fur remains is brittle and discolored.

Algie looks up at her mother and asks, "Mama, why didn't you get one of the cabbies to help you? He could have bitten you."

"I don't need no help. I can take care of myself!"

Algie walks around the dog to get a better look. Champ rolls his head towards her and emits a soft whimper.

"Take it easy boy. Just let me get a closer look." Algie puts her hands behind her and stares down at Champ's bald spots. She looks up at her mother again, but this time with a frown. "Mama, this isn't rabies! This dog has got mange."

Suddenly, they hear a loud noise coming from the house next door! Both women look over and see Miss Adele running down her stairs toward Algie and Champ.

"What's the matter? Is Champ hurt?" Miss Adele's voice is full of grief and fear.

"He's OK, Miss Adele," Algie reassures her. "Champ is just fine. My mother got confused. If you hold him, I can get this helmet off his head."

Miss Adele bends down and places both her arms firmly and lovingly around Champ. Algie is able to easily remove the helmet from the relieved dog's head.

"Miss Adele, do you know your dog has mange?"

"Yes, I do. I got some ointment to put on it. Is that why she put a helmet on his head?"

"I'm afraid so, my mother thought he had rabies."

"Rabies! No! No! Champ does not have rabies! He's not foaming at the mouth or running crazy down the street in cold sweat!"

Miss Adele releases her beloved pet and he hobbles as fast as he can pass the women, up the stairs, and into the open front door.

"Sorry, Miss Adele, it was a bad mistake. Glad you got medicine for Champ. Hope he's better real soon."

"It's alright Algie. But next time, just come get me if you think something's wrong with him. I'll take care of it. I'll take care of it right away."

"Yes, Miss Adele. We surely will."

Miss Adele returns to her house and Algie climbs the stairs, carrying the helmet. She walks past her mother and returns the helmet to its place on the porch. Chauncey follows Algie into the house and puts the broom back in the kitchen. She pinches a big piece of snuff from her tin and lies back in her chair, closing her eyes. "I still say it's the rabies," she blurts out into the empty room.

Algie is in the bedroom and pretends not to hear her.

When Algie returns to The Place, Tressie is feeling sick and asks to leave early. Dodd can't pick her up until he gets off, so she goes to the house to lie down. As Tressie leaves, a black sedan pulls up and parks in front of Clover's. It's early in the afternoon, so there are only a couple of patrons inside who are playing dominoes. The two white men, in matching charcoal gray suits, walk nonchalantly into the pool room as if it they are regulars. The men playing dominoes look up from their game. Crook is at the bar, his back to the men, cleaning shot glasses.

"Willie Clover?" The older of the two men is the first to speak.

Crook is surprised to see white men in his place. Even Frisch stands outside. "Yes. I'm Willie Clover. What can I do for you gentlemen?"

"Just need to ask you a few questions." The older man continues.

"Sure, sure, how can I help you?"

The younger man leans against the bar, while the older man begins the interrogation. "How long you been running this place, Mr. Clover?"

"About six years. I haven't had any trouble here. May I ask who you are and why you gentlemen need to know that?"

The two agents ignore his questions.

"How many employees do you have?" The younger man poses this question.

Crook does not immediately answer. These aren't cops, but they're sure trying to act like they are. His mind is racing. Who are these guys? He's paid Frisch for the month. Crook takes a few minutes to calm his rattled nerves and decides to do a little fishing of his own. "Who are you with? Are you with the police?"

The two men glance at each other, and the younger agent stands up from the bar.

"No, Mr. Clover we aren't. But we're with the government."

"Really? Which outfit you with?"

Again, the men glance at each other.

"We just want to ask you a few questions, Mr. Clover. There's no reason for you to get defensive," says the older man.

"I just want to know what this is all about. I pay my rent and I run a clean, quiet place. I'm not defensive. I just need to know why you here, so I can tell you what you want to know."

The older agent steps closer towards Crook. He uses both hands to motion for him to calm down. The agent then places his hands, palms down, on the bar. In a loud whisper he asks, "Mr. Clover, do you serve liquor in here?"

So, that's it. Who told it? There's no way he can hide the bottles now. "Like I said, I run a clean place. I think we can handle this in an easy, quiet way."

"Do you serve liquor in here, Mr. Clover?" The younger agent, who is now standing next to his partner, repeats the question.

Perspiration is beading on Crook's forehead. His hands are wet and he's fighting the urge to run out the back door.

"Mind if we have a look?" asks the older agent, as he walks around the counter.

Crook steps aside and says nothing.

The agent bends down and counts the bottles. "Mr. Clover, do you know it's illegal to sell liquor without a license?"

Crook doesn't reply.

"We're going to have to shut you down," announces the younger agent.

All three men jump when a chair hits the floor. The two domino players have abandoned their game, cursing and wrestling each other to be the first one out the front door.

"Gentlemen, surely we can work this out?" Sweat is now pouring down Crook's face.

"And, how would we do that, Mr. Clover?" asks the older agent.

"W-w-well, what I mean is," says Crook who is now stuttering. "I-I-I contribute to the community and I-I-I provide a place for working men to enjoy themselves without getting into any trouble. I don't want my place shut down. What's it gonna take?"

Both men look down at the counter and then, simultaneously, look up to stare at Crook.

"Are you trying to bribe us?" asks the younger man.

Crook doesn't know what to say. The only sound in the room is the ticking clock on the wall.
"Yes, or no. Are you offering us a bribe, Mr. Clover?"

Crook is caught. Are they going for it or are they setting him up for more charges? He stares at the bar counter and wipes his soaking wet palms back-and-forth across the top. "I guess that's up to you."

Again, silence.

The younger agent clicks his teeth and his partner follows him to the middle of the room. The two talk softly and Crook doesn't bother to try to hear what they're saying. After several minutes, the older agent walks back over to the counter, the younger man behind him.

"We're not extortionists, Mr. Clover," he begins. "We provide a public service. Therefore, we're going to give you an opportunity to purchase a license directly from us."

Crook understands the game now. "How long is this license good for?"

"About three months, Mr. Clover. You'll need to renew it every three months," explains the younger agent.

Crook slowly nods his head, sealing the deal on the shakedown.

The younger man is already at the door. At the same time, four cabbies are coming into Clover's. All stare with concern and curiosity at the two departing white men.

"We'll get back in-touch with you soon, Mr. Clover," yells the older agent, as the two men leave the poolroom.

"What was that all about?" asks one of the cabbies.

"Nothing man. They work for Frisch, the man that owns this building. They was talking about some renovations and what it would cost."

His answer satisfies the cabbies and the four men sit down for a game spades.

Crook pulls a towel from behind the counter and dries the sweat from his face, neck, and hands. He wonders: Who told on me? Not the fellows, my stuff's cheaper than Benny's across the street. Not Frisch. He never even comes into my place. Who else are they trying to shake down? Benny? Flamingo's? Algie?

Algie looks away as Crook comes into The Place. She's working a crossword puzzle in the newspaper. She saw the cars and the white men through the window, and she already knows why they were there.

"Algie, did those white men come in here?"

"No, Crook. They did not. What did they want?"

"Nothing, nothing; something about renovations Frisch wants to do. They didn't say nothing to you about it?"

"No, Crook they didn't. What kind of renovations is Mr. Frisch planning to do?

"I don't know, they didn't say. I was just checking to see what they said to you?"

Algie finally looks at Crook and says, "Like, I said, they didn't come in here."

Without a goodbye, Crook leaves and crosses the street over to Benny's Bar.

In the white margin above her puzzle, Algie writes the words: MAYBE NOW YOU WILL STAY OUT OF MY BUSINESS!

Before she can get back to her crossword, however, Early comes through the door.

"Hey babe! What's new?"

Algie pours him a cup of coffee and asks, "How was the job?"

"OK. Nothing much. He just wanted some sticks and leaves cleared from his backyard."

She places the cup in front of Early and he begins sipping the hot coffee. Algie resumes working her puzzle, but is bothered by the sound of a soft sizzle coming from the kitchen, just as Benny comes through the door.

"Afternoon, Algie."

Algie acknowledges Benny's greeting with a broad smile as she hurries into the kitchen to see what might be spilling over.

"You ready for lunch Benny?"

"Sure, but what I really came over here for was to talk to you about Crook. He just left my place."

"Yes, I know. He was just over here, too. He said two white men came into the pool room to discuss some renovations Frisch is planning for the building."

As Algie prepares his lunch, Benny and Early politely ignore each other. They listen in silence as Algie works in the kitchen. Within a few minutes, she returns with Benny's lunch, a decision he always leaves up to her. This time, it's a BLT sandwich, an order of "hot" fries, and a cold bottle of RC.

Benny wants to discuss Crook's visitors, but not with Early around. Algie wants to talk, too, but will wait for Early to leave, too.

The smiles and glances between Algie and Benny have not gone unnoticed by Early. Although he continues sipping his coffee, he's angry that she didn't offer him lunch, too. He glances down at a new *Watchtower* lying on the counter. The magazine is opened to a page titled, "Did not Lucifer become Satan the Devil, according to Isaiah 14:12?" Early picks up the magazine. He recognizes the names Lucifer and Satan, but he doesn't know who Isaiah might be. To no one in particular, he says, "God made Satan for a reason and folks just need to 'cept that."

Benny licks the sweet, hot sauce from his fries off his fingers and replies, "God did not create Satan. The devil created himself."

Algie is concentrating on the puzzle, but anxious for Early to finish his coffee and leave.

Early slurps the last drop of his coffee and turns in his seat to face Benny. "God made the devil so people would know what's good and what's evil!"

Benny pulls a paper napkin from the dispenser, wipes his hands, and now turns in his seat towards Early. "People do not need Satan in order to know the difference between good and bad," Benny explains, using a precise, affected tone. "Adam and Eve did that for us."

"Mister Thomas," continues Early, trying to mimic Benny's voice. "It says in the bible that the Devil showed Adam and Eve right from wrong when he got her to eat that apple in the Garden of Eden."

"If you could read the Bible, Mr. Bird, you would know that it was the tree in the middle of the Garden of Eden that taught Adam and Eve, good from evil. It was called the tree of the knowledge of good and bad. Satan or no Satan, if Adam and Eve stayed away from the tree, then that was good. If they ate from the tree, then that was bad."

Early bristles. True, he's had little education, but the Bible is one book he knows a little something about. The slight doesn't go unnoticed by Algie either. She stares at Benny and slightly shakes her head at him. It's too much for Benny. He can deal with Early's ignorance, but how can Algie sit here and defend this fool?

"If Satan hadn't of spoke to Eve, they would never had touched the tree! So, the devil is still the reason they learned right from wrong."

Algie has had enough. She slides the magazine off the counter onto her lap. She hopes the gesture will end the conversation that is obviously more a reason to fight than a real disagreement.

"No sir, Mr. Bird, the tree was there first! Satan came later. The devil may be a killer, but Adam and Eve made the decision to sin and die."
"Early are you finished with your coffee?" asks Algie, a little too loudly, trying to distract both men.

Early ignores her and walks over to Benny's stool. "Who died and put you in charge of the bible, Reverend Thomas? Last time I checked, you was a saloon owner and I don't see no bibles sitting on them tables across the street!"

Benny slams his fist down on the counter and stands up to face Early. The two are standing so close, Early can smell the bacon on Benny's breath, and Benny can smell the coffee Early just finished. "At least I own a business and have a steady income! I'm not sitting around here in this woman's restaurant waiting for a job to come to me!"

Early jerks his head to the side and flashes a tight smile, pressing his teeth together so hard that his gums are beginning to hurt. But before he can reply, Algie throws her body across the counter between the two men. Benny and Early jerk back to allow her room. Early bursts out laughing, but Benny drops his head in shame.

"That's enough!" With her body still extended over the counter, she addresses Early first. "Early Bird, don't you need to go next door?" He stops laughing. He feels like a little boy whose mother has just told him to excuse himself from the dinner table. He leaves and doesn't look back. Algie turns to Benny. "Benny Thomas, was that really necessary?"

Benny sits back down and finishes eating his now cold bacon sandwich. Algie pulls herself off the counter and back into her stool. Benny takes a couple of long swigs of RC and then pushes the plate and pop to the side. He folds his arms across his chest and stares at the wall behind her.

Algie knows he's upset, but she needs to talk about the white men that were at Crook's. She pours two cups of coffee and places one cup in front of Benny, who pretends not to notice. She then pulls her stool down the counter, facing him. She begins sipping her coffee and, after a few minutes, Benny begins to drink from his cup. Now she can ask him, "What did Crook tell you about those two white men?"

"Not much. Just wanted to know if they had come by my place? Did they come over here, too?"

"No, they didn't. Crook asked me the same thing. Did he tell you what they wanted?"

"Nope. But, I get the feeling he's scared. He said somebody is talking out-of-turn and putting his business in the street. I didn't know what he was talking about."

Benny gets up to leave and Algie goes back into the kitchen.

Early is still sulking. He knows Benny is at The Place all the time; enough folks have told him about it. At first, that didn't bother him too much. After all, Benny's Bar is across the street and The Place is the closest restaurant. But, when he found out the barkeeper was sometimes walking Algie home in the evenings, he became angry and asked her about it. To his surprise, she didn't deny or even try to hide it. True, their relationship is more social than romantic, but there are certain rules every couple should abide by and he told her so.

Algie listened but gave him no reassurances, and she did not tell him that she would not allow Benny to see her home in the evenings. Early thought she would suggest that he accompany her, but she didn't.

Most evenings he's gambling in the alley. Algie doesn't know and doesn't need to, as far as he sees it. She gets most of what's left of his government check after rent and money for Screamie.
That evening, a few customers are dining in at The Place, but most are picking up orders to-go. It's busy, but not all at once, so Algie can handle it alone without Tressie.

She propped the door open to let in some much needed air; it's still quite warm for this time of year. It's Wednesday, so the House of Faith is holding choir practice. In between customers, Algie listens to the chords stop-and-start as the singers rehearse for Sunday. The song she now hears is familiar and it reminds her of Dublin. She begins softly singing along.

> *Do you have good religion?*
> (*chorus*): Certainly, Lord.
> *Do you have good religion?*
> (*chorus*): Certainly, Lord.
> *Do you have good religion?*
> (*chorus*): Certainly, Lord. Certainly. Certainly. Certainly Looord!

Grandma Julia had been the main soloist at the one-room church Algie attended as a child. Chauncey never went to church and Grandma Julia told her it was a sin to blame God for her dead babies. Chauncey asked her mother to pray for her, because she wouldn't be coming to pray for herself.

Algie liked going to church with Grandma Julia, a woman who was well respected, popular, and had a beautiful singing voice. She laughs to herself remembering the name of the church that had a title longer than the front door: "Church of the Rock of His Blessed Pasturage of the Lamb's Eternal Light".

Grandma Julia hated that name, "too showy" she complained. Everyone just called it Lamb's Light, except the church's self-anointed and self-appointed pastor who claims the name came to him in a dream.

Unlike Chauncey, Grandma Julia's other children did attend the church. All of them are dead now, except for Chauncey and Uncle Gabriel, who is 84 years old and still lives in Dublin.

Algie has a multitude of cousins and recalls many happy gatherings with them for birthdays, holidays, and summer picnics. A few cousins are still in Georgia, but most of them have come north, too. Unfortunately, none relocated to Dayton. The majority went to Detroit, others went to New York, and Uncle Ezra's kids are all in California. Algie is in touch with her cousin Georgia, one of Aunt Florence's daughters, who lives in Detroit. Georgia sends a Christmas card every year and never misses Algie's birthday on July 18th. In kind, Algie returns the favor, never forgetting to send a card for Georgia's birthday or the holidays.

Algie's memories are interrupted when she hears a familiar voice coming from the House of Faith. She again sings along, filling in the words the soloist has forgotten or doesn't know.

> *If every you need him, just pray.*
> (*chorus*): Just pray.
> *He'll lead you and, uhm, uhm, the way.*
> (*chorus*): Show you the way.
> *Whenever you have doubts*
> *And don't know what life's all about*
> *Call on God to uhm, uhm...*
> (*chorus*): Save the day.

Algie is annoyed. It's such a beautiful song. Why can't Viola remember the words? She jumps up from her seat. "That's Viola!" she shouts out loud. She looks around the restaurant and sees a customer sitting at a table finishing up his meal. Algie tells him she needs to step out for a minute, but if he doesn't mind, "Would you let any customer that comes in know I'll be right back in a minute?" The man is agreeable; he's in no hurry.

The doors of the church are wide open, so Algie walks right in and sees Viola swaying from side-to-side in her choir robe, trying to finish her solo. Algie takes a seat and waits for her to finish. Viola's voice is not exceptional, but the tone is pleasant. She stumbles over several of the words and tries to make up for it with a theatrical flair that includes raising her eyebrows and rolling her lips with each note. Viola raises her arms for every crescendo, and then slowly brings them back down like a fluttering butterfly.

After several starts and stops, the song finally ends. Algie stands and motions for Viola to come over; the latter is all smiles. "You didn't know I could sing. Did you?"

"No, Viola, I didn't. But why are you singing over here? Are you leaving Mt. Moriah?"

"Oh, no Mom. I'm just over here practicing. I'm going to do a solo at our anniversary celebration."

"Well congratulations! I'm very happy for you Viola. But shouldn't you be practicing with your own choir at Mt. Moriah?"

Viola stops smiling. "Let's just say the Lord works in mysterious ways."

Just then, Norma Jean and Gloria walk up behind Viola. Algie hadn't seen them when she came in. She nods a "hello" to both women, who flank Viola like trained guard dogs.

"I was just congratulating Viola on her solo, but wondering why you're over here practicing." Algie repeats the statement, hoping one of the Collins sisters will tell her more.

Norma Jean steps forward and wraps her huge palms around Algie's right hand, completely encasing it. "Miss Algie, so good to see you again. I know that you're proud of your daughter, and so are we. We're here at the House of Faith so Viola can have the privacy she needs to get ready for our special occasion. The choir at Mt. Moriah is so large and so many songs are being planned. We thought it better to rehearse here. The Rev. Peters was okay with it, especially since Viola is one of your daughters and he treasures his friendship with you."

Algie smiles at Norma Jean, but gives Viola a puzzled look. What is going on? What are these bulls and Viola up to? Something isn't right and Algie knows it. She eases her hand out of Norma Jean's grasp and encourages Viola to keep practicing. She tells the trio she must return to the restaurant and makes them promise to stop by for diner when rehearsals are completed.

Algie walks back to The Place, troubled. Something's wrong. No good will come from that solo.

A customer is standing at the counter and Algie apologies for the wait as she takes the young woman's order. She didn't notice Benny, at first, since he was sitting on the stool at the far end of the counter. He nods at her and tells her to go ahead, he can wait. Algie prepares the order, wraps it to-go, and hands it to the woman.

"It's too early for dinner. What brings you back so soon?"

With his head bowed, Benny replies, "Algie, I came back to apologize. I shouldn't have argued with Early like that. I know he means a lot to you and my behavior wasn't right. I hope we're still friends?"

"Benny Thomas, you and I will always be friends."

Benny slowly looks up and smiles. "OK, Miss Algie. I was just making sure. Well, I need to get back to the bar." He walks briskly across the street and looks back at The Place so many times, that he trips over his feet twice. Through the window, Algie watches Benny stumbling and smiling.

When she met Early, her intention was to help out a nice young man who was down on his luck. Algie thought he might even be a good match for Viola or Honey. Then, Early brought Screamie, a red-haired baby like one she had always hoped to have with Edward. Cashing Early's checks, paying his bills, and handling his mail is a small price for time with Screamie. She doubts Benny would understand any of this, but knows there will come a time when she will have to let Screamie and Edward go for good.

FIVE

It's now August 1, 1958. Tressie is pregnant again. She's in her seventh month and the pregnancy has been going well. As she is walking out the door of the House of Faith on this hot, cloudless Sunday, she is annoyed to feel sweat trickling down her legs. Before Tressie reaches for the car door, pain rips across her underbelly and drags her to the ground. She falls forward and leans against the door. She can't cry for help, barely able to draw a breath. That's all she remembers.

Twenty-four hours later, when she finally awakens, Tressie is alone in a hospital room. The bed next to her is empty. She looks down at her deflated stomach and bites her lower lip, causing it to bleed. The nurse returns to take her temperature and checks her blood pressure. Moments later, a red-eyed Dodd comes in and sits in a chair near her bed. He takes her hand, but can offer no words of comfort.

Tressie and Dodd name their baby girl, who lived a mere three hours, Treasure. They hadn't named their six-hour-old son, but that was before Tressie learned from her *Watchtower* that they would live again. This time, they paid for a casket and a plot at Green Castle Cemetery. Rev. Peters said the eulogy at the graveside service. Tressie only wanted the immediate family there, and they all came — except Viola.

It's been a month since the death of Treasure and Algie continues to work alone at The Place. Tressie is physically fine, but unable to work — no focus, no energy, and, this time, no hope. Honey and Bo help Algie on the weekends and some evenings, too. Viola, however, has become scarce. Honey eventually confronted Viola about not helping out at The Place, but the latter always insists she has somewhere else she needs to be.

Honey and Bo have been together since Honey was stabbed. Bo never asked about the woman and Honey didn't offer an explanation. It's all in the past. Every Sunday they eat dinner together at The Place, after they finish helping Algie.

This Sunday Viola shows up, bringing with her a new, silk scarf that has bright, green, four-leaf clovers scattered haphazardly across a white background. She is pulling her new scarf on-and-off her shoulders; tying it around her head and then removing it to make a bow around her neck. Just as quickly, she unties the bow and swirls the scarf into her lap like a napkin.

Despite the theatrics, Algie refuses to ask about the scarf. She picks up Screamie and walks around the counter. The child reaches for Viola's scarf, but can't get it. With Screamie riding on her hip, Algie opens the door, but stops to look back when she hears Honey laughing.

"Mom, look who's coming for dinner," says Honey.

Algie turns around and can't believe her eyes either. Chauncey is standing on the sidewalk, wearing her heavy coat, hat, and boots, and carrying a suitcase. With more than a little effort, Chauncey manages to maneuver the heavy piece of luggage through the door and sets it down in front of Algie.

Viola begins cackling like a crazed hen. Honey is laughing so hard, she can barely stand. Screamie buries her face in Algie's shoulder, frightened by all the loud laughter.

"Mama, what are you doing here? And where do you think you're going?"

"She's finally lost all of her mind," says Viola, as she ties the scarf around her waist like a belt.

Bo remains quiet, unsure if it's okay for him to laugh, too. Honey's laughter, however, has reached hysteria. She's leaning to one side, both arms behind her back, trying to keep from falling completely over.

"How did you get down here? Did you walk by yourself? Algie continues her line of questioning, but pauses to silence Viola and Honey with a threatening: "Both of you, be quiet!"

Viola licks her lips and Honey sits down, before she falls down.

"Mama, where are you going in a coat and hat in this heat?

"She probably decided to set out for hell on her own," says Viola. "Even Satan won't come around here to get her!"

Chauncey is visibly shaken and breathless. The short journey has worn her out. She manages to finally say, "I'm going home."

"Ha! Like I said!" laughs Viola.

"Viola April Clover, I'm not going to tell you again," says Algie. "One more word and I am going to stick that scarf some place you won't be able to retrieve it!"

Bo coughs to clear the laugh from his throat; his dimples

burrowing deeper into his cheeks. Honey covers her face with both hands and leans against Bo.

"Mama, where are you going?"

"I'm going home."

"Mama, come over here and sit down."

Chauncey drops into the chair next to Bo. Algie hands Screamie to Honey and then gets a cup of coffee for Chauncey. She sets the steaming cup on the table in front of her mother.

"Mama, what is this all about? What made you decide to go home today?"

Chauncey sips her coffee and takes her time before answering. "I'm ready to go home. I came around here to ask you for bus fare. You said you would help me go home whenever I was ready. Well, I'm ready to go now."

"Did something happen at home?"

"Don't matter! I'm ready to go home. You're not going to burn me up like a slab of pork rib and then throw me to the wind!"

Viola and Honey exchange amused looks. Honey covers her mouth. Algie is bewildered. Chauncey has never left the front yard, and why is she talking about being burned up?

"Mama, who have you been talking to?"

"Like I said, I'm ready to go home."

"Well, if you ask me," begins Viola again. But she stops short when she sees her mother's angry forefinger pointed in her direction.

Bo wants to leave; clearly, this is a family matter and his presence won't help the situation. He excuses himself saying, "I hate that Clover's is closed on Sundays. I could go over there to get out of the way of you ladies, instead I …" Before he can finish his sentence, Algie stands up, causing Honey to step backwards and stumble over her own feet, almost losing her grip on Screamie.

"Mama has Crook been around to the house?"

Chauncey looks at Algie and smugly replies, "Maybe he has."

"Mama has Crook been to the house or not!"

"Yeah, he come by and he told me how you planning to get rid of me. That's why you don't want to go back to Dublin."

"Mama, no one has plans to get rid of you. Tell me exactly what Crook said."

Chauncey stares into the empty coffee cup. "Crook came by the house after you left this morning. He wanted to know if you had gotten the letter from Mr. Snell. I told him you did and showed him the letter. He asked me what we were going to do about it. I told him it was up to you, but that I thought we should take Mr. Snell up on his offer."

Viola smirks, but says nothing. Honey, on the other hand, stares at her mother with her mouth wide open. "What? Mr. Snell? You mean that plantation owner in Georgia. Mom, what you writing him for?

"I didn't write to him Honey, he wrote a letter to me. Now sit and be quiet, so I can get the whole story from your grandmother. Go ahead Mama. Finish telling me what happened."

"Crook told me he knew the reason why you didn't want to go back. You can get a bunch of insurance money for putting me down like a dog. Then you can burn me into ashes so you won't have to pay for a funeral. He said you're in deep debt trying to run this restaurant. So you took out that insurance on me to save yourself."

"That's not true," says Honey, before Algie can respond. "Grandma, that's a bald-faced lie!"

Algie sighs deeply. "Bo, would you mind driving my mother back around to the house?"

"Ahn, ahn, no ma'am," says Chauncey. "I'm going back home today!"

"Yes, you are going home; right around to 254 Dunbar Avenue. Honey give Screamie to Viola and help your grandmother into the car. Bo, please carry her suitcase."

Viola takes the child and promptly places her on the mat behind the counter.

Algie prepares a plate of food for her mother. Bo picks up the suitcase, but Chauncey remains in her seat. She refuses to stand, despite Honey's urgings.

Algie returns with the plate and gently pushes Honey to the side. She leans over and kisses her mother on the forehead and says, "Mama, Bo and Honey are going to get you back home where it's safe. I made a plate of dinner for you. So, go on home and forget about Crook's lies."

Chauncey looks up at her daughter through watery eyes. She's tired and scared. Chauncey rises from the chair and Honey and Bo help her out the door and into the car. Algie watches the car's taillights disappear around the corner onto Fitch Street. She looks in the opposite direction and sees a group of House of Faith parishioners headed her way, coming for their Sunday dinner.

The Sunday crowd is moderate and Algie is grateful. By closing time, she's physically and emotionally spent. As she's cleaning up for the night, the door opens. She's mopping the floor with her back to the door. "Sorry, we're closed."

Hearing no response, she stops mopping and turns around and sees a ghost from the past — Mazy.

"Mazy, is that you?" Algie drops the mop and rushes to hug the equally excited woman walking into The Place. She and Mazy became friends at Lamb's Light. The girls first met in Sunday school when Algie was 11 years old, and Mazy was 6. The two were immediately drawn to each other and Mazy always insisted on sitting next to Algie. Grandma Julia told Algie that Mazy was her sister, but to keep it quiet or Chauncey would have a fit.

"Algie Julia, you look the same!"

"So, do you! Come over here and take a seat. How did you get here? Why didn't you call to let me know you were coming?"

The two women sit smiling at each other, just like than did at Lamb's Light.

"I'm living with my son, Floyd. Right here in Dayton, Ohio. I came a little over a year ago, but I didn't have an address for you. I told my son I was sure this is where you moved, but of course, he didn't know you back in Dublin."

"So, how did you find me?"

"Well, Floyd's buddy brought him over here one weekend to

Clover's next door. The next day he mentioned the name of the place to me. I asked him, 'How many Clovers could there be in Dayton?' He came back the next weekend and spoke with the owner, who told him you were right next door. We meant to come sooner, but my son has a crazy work schedule."

"Is your son with you? "Where is he?"

"He's waiting in the car outside."

"Tell him to come in."

Mazy grabs Algie's hand and pulls her back into her seat. "No, no. I'm only going to be a minute. He wants to stay in the car."

Algie sits back down and squeezes her sister's hand. "I'm just so happy you found me! I was cleaning up, but I can get a meal together for you and your son."

"No, don't bother. You've worked all day and I've had my dinner. Now that I know where you are, I can get Floyd to bring me back anytime."

The two sisters sit for a moment and just smile at one another, happy to again be in each other's company. Mazy breaks the comfortable silence to ask about Viola. Algie frowns. "Viola is Viola. She looks more like him than you, and I suspect she's got more of his personality, too!"

Mazy laughs. "Have you ever told her about me?"

"No, we didn't tell her. No reason, we just didn't. And what good would it do now?"

Mazy nods in agreement. "I was just so grateful that you and Eddie Mack took her. I knew she was in good hands."

Mazy gave birth to Viola when she was 14 years old. The father of the infant was a friend of Berry's, who had been abusing her since she was 11 years old. When her pregnancy was discovered and Mazy identified her rapist, her father left the house. Berry didn't return for three days. When he did come back, he said nothing about his whereabouts or what he had done while he was away. His former friend, Viola's biological father, was never seen or heard from again.

When the baby was born, Mazy's mother wanted to keep her. She named the child Viola after her own sister, but Berry wouldn't allow it. Everyone in Dublin knew about the child and how she had been conceived — including Edward and Algie. During that time, Algie had just lost a baby, a son. She was still in her sick bed when Edward brought the baby girl to her.

"I'd like to see her sometime Algie. And you know I won't say a word about her beginnings."

"She still lives at home with me and is in-and-out of the restaurant all the time. I'll arrange it."

"Well, let me get out of your way." Mazy gets up to leave.

"You just got here!"

"Yes, I know sis, but Floyd is waiting in the car and, like I said, he has a crazy work schedule.

Write down your address and phone number first." Algie pulls the little pad she uses for orders from her pocket. Mazy writes down the information and the two women embrace, promising to get in-touch again soon.

Chauncey had opposed the adoption. Therefore, Edward and Algie had to vigilantly shield their new daughter from

Chauncey's outbursts and slights. Chauncey would call 6-year-old Tressie over to give her an apple or some other little treat. Four-year-old Viola would come looking for the same treat or affection, but was shooed away as if she were the house pet. Algie would immediately take the treat from Tressie and give half to Viola, explaining to her girls that sharing was the best way of showing love. She would often stop, too, in the middle of whatever she was doing, to sit and cuddle with Viola in clear view of Chauncey. But of course, she couldn't be everywhere and she could always tell when Viola had been hurt by Chauncey.

By the time Viola began school, however, Chauncey's attitude towards her had softened. Algie could find no explanation for it, but Edward attributed it to dirt saying, "A mouthful of Georgia red clay will make crazy do right."

Edward had deferred to Algie when it came to dealing with her mother. But before Viola's fifth birthday, he decided to put an end to her nasty remarks and bad attitude toward his middle daughter. His child would soon start school and with that learning, Viola would become fully aware of the differences her grandmother made between her and her sisters.

One Sunday, after Algie and the girls had gone to church, Edward approached Chauncey as she sat on the front porch dipping snuff and drinking coffee. At first, he tried reasoning with her, appealing to her as a grandmother and reminding her of the sons he and Algie lost. Agitated, Chauncey stood facing him and waved her arms wildly; cursing and spitting snuff. For the "umpteenth time", she reminded him, "you stole my daughter. And now you want us to accept this bastard born to a 13-year-old whore."

Edward let Chauncey have her say, but finally her tirade exhausted his patience. He let loose a verbal riptide that concluded with a truth she had self-righteously failed to mention.

"And last, but not least, your only daughter was gotten and born in sin, too. You were married to Willie Jordan when you laid down like a swamp whore for Berry Smith!" Chauncey balled that insult into a fist and swung at Edward with all her might, catching him just under the chin. The punch caused him to lose his balance, but he still managed to deliver a slap across her cheek that sent her face down into the hard, red Georgia clay. Edward left her there and drove away in his truck.

When Algie got home, Chauncey was in bed. She worriedly told Edward her mother must be ill, but won't say what's wrong. Algie kept trying to tend to Chauncey's illness, but was angrily shooed away. Chauncey remained in bed for a week. When she rejoined the family, she'd made up her mind to shun all her granddaughters.

Algie puts the mop away, swings her purse over her shoulder, and begins the walk home. The night sky is cloudless and a full moon lights her way. Like a sleepwalker, Algie dreams the streets turn into winter fields, waiting for the first signs of spring. The rush of a passing cab sounds like Georgia pines shivering in the wind. The leaves crackling beneath her feet are burning kindling that fills the air all around her. Did she just hear the night call of a Whippoorwill? Is that a possum shuffling through the brush? Algie can't make the memories of home come, but when they do, she doesn't fight it. Instead, she wraps her mind and heart around Dublin and doesn't let go until the memories let go of her.

As she opens the door, she decides not to mention Mazy's visit to Chauncey, especially not today. She's relieved to find her already asleep in bed and dear, sweet Honey asleep in a chair next to her. She pours herself a glass of cold milk and sits at the kitchen table.

A wave of sadness sweeps over her and she shudders at the thought of where Viola's latest sin offering — that clover-covered scarf — might have come from.

The next day, Algie decides to rest. Generally, on Mondays, she works through a list of chores and waits for Honey to get home from work to drive her around town. Honey works a half-day on Mondays, specifically for Algie to go shopping, to the bank — wherever she needs to go. This Monday, however, Algie just wants to rest.

After her bath, she puts on a housecoat and joins a quiet and subdued Chauncey in the living room. The radio is on; the heavy static is background noise. Neither woman is listening anyway; a malaise hangs over both of them. They sit for a long time until a knock on the front door jolts them out of their stupors. The delivery man and his assistant carefully place a large, corrugated box just inside the front door.

"What's that?" asks Chauncey.

Algie looks at the dark, block letters and reads: Zenith Television. "It's a TV."

"A TV? What made you go out and buy that?"

"I didn't buy it. Apparently, Honey did."

"Where you planning to put it? You can't leave it sitting at the front door like that."

"It can sit here for now. When Honey gets in, she'll decide where to put it."

Algie returns to the couch, but Chauncey gets up to inspect the box. She can't read the words, but is obviously intrigued by the package. She likes the fact that there will be a TV in the house, but doesn't say it. Back in Dublin, the first TV she saw was in the home of a family she cleaned for; she stole glances at the moving images as she went about her work.

Algie watches her mother, watching the box. She sees the satisfaction on her face, and then, it happens, Chauncey smiles.

When Honey got home, she squealed and jumped with joy. She had purchased the TV as a surprise and she's pleased at their appreciation for the big, brown box. Honey calls Bo with the news and he'll be over after work to set it up. In the meantime, the three women try to decide on the best spot for the TV. Their conversation is excited and animated. Algie is beaming at this rare moment that has brought a smile to all three of their faces. She only wishes that Viola were here, too.

On Tuesday, Algie is still in an especially happy mood. She's just finishing a fried fish sandwich for a lunch order when a messenger walks into The Place. Algie gives the teenager a nickel and stares at the flimsy paper. She's never seen a telegram before. As she hands the cabbie George his lunch, she asks him to stop next door at Crook's and tell Early to step over for a minute.

"What you need babe?"

"This telegram just came for you."

"A telegram? For me? What does it say?

Algie does not read the message back to him verbatim, but informs him that his mother wants him to come home immediately.

"For what? Is somebody sick?"

"It's not clear. It just says there's a family emergency and you need to get there right away." Algie hands the telegram to him.

Early accepts Algie's explanation, but is bothered by the request. He's never told her the real reason why he hasn't returned home to Sweetwater, Texas, and emergency aside, he doesn't want to go now.

In Sweetwater, Early delivered illegal booze to local joints and bars for a man called Crackers. He thought Crackers was too stingy and wasn't paying him enough money for the risks he was taking. So, Early decided to increase the liquor supply and keep the extra profits. He would pick up the bottled liquor from Crackers and take it home to his mother's house. He would then redistribute the liquor into identical bottles half filled with water and soda. After he had made the arranged deliveries, he would sell the excess bottles independently, pocketing the money.

When Crackers found out, he came looking for Early with a rifle. The latter took a bus to Abilene, about 50 miles away, and joined the army. He hasn't been back to Texas since.

Early now turns the telegram over and over in his hands. He has never seen one either and he wonders who sent it. His mother can barely write and she doesn't know anything about sending a message like this. He sits down on a stool at the counter and silently fingers the paper. It's his business, so Algie decides not to try to advise Early. She can't tell what's worrying him more, receiving the telegram or the thought of going home.

Bo and Benny come into The Place together. They sit at the counter, away from Early. They're in a deep conversation about a book that Bo brought with him. Algie returns from the kitchen, where she's already started Benny's lunch, and asks Bo what he would like. He tells her a tuna sandwich with coleslaw. The two men continue their conversation even after Algie brings out their lunches.

Early folds the telegram and puts it in his back pocket. Despite his trepidation, he's decided to buy a bus ticket. He'll leave on Wednesday and be back in a week. He tells Algie his decision and leaves The Place.

"What's that book about?" asks Algie.

Bo speaks up first. "It's called *The Invisible Man*[5]." The writer is trying to explain why black men like me and Benny are invisible to the world."

"Invisible? I can see both of you clear as day."

Bo and Benny laugh with Algie.

"No, not that kind of invisible, Miss Algie," says Bo. "He means we're not recognized as men, but rather they think of us as stereotypes; dumb, uneducated, clownish buffoons."

"Whose it by?"

"Ralph Ellison," answers Benny. "I've never read it, but I heard about it. Bo is like a walking library. He knows all about these new black writers."

Bo smiles with appreciation at Benny. He's no expert, but he does have a voracious appetite for reading. "I've always loved to read Miss Algie. But my reading only began to have an effect on my life when I discovered how important these times are for us as a people. There are so many books now written by us and for us. They tell our history and even predict our future."

"Listen to him Algie," says Benny with pride. "He sounds like a college professor, don't he?"

---

[5] *The Invisible Man* by Ralph Ellison won the National Book Award in 1953.

"Yes, he does and there's nothing wrong with that." Although she can read and write fairly well, Algie has always admired people who can read and understand fine books. That is, books bound in leather and trimmed in gold. This book doesn't look like that, but from what Bo said about it, the words could certainly be stored inside such precious pages. Maybe Bo's love of books and learning will rub-off on Honey. Even if it doesn't, it would be a blessing for her to be the wife of such a man.

Algie takes her seat on the stool and leaves the two men to their meal and man-talk.

Benny, however, is only half-listening. He heard Early talking to Algie and then put the telegram away. What's going on? Maybe, it's the message that will send Early away for good.

SIX

Algie still works alone at The Place. She feels even lonelier whenever she looks over to Screamie's vacant mat. As she scans the Sunday newspaper and sips her second cup of coffee, a light snow begins to fall; the temperature has dropped 20 degrees in the last hour. Winter has finally arrived. The Sunday dinners are cooking on the stove, waiting for the House of Faith services to end. The sounds of praise from the church are barely audible; the cold has forced the congregation to keep the windows closed.

Algie goes to check the food and hears a car door shut. It's Viola. Algie looks at her watch. "What are you doing here so early?"

Viola walks around the counter and pours herself a cup of coffee. "Left service early today Mama. It's cold and I'm not feeling 100 percent."

"What's wrong? Do you feel like a cold's coming on?"

"Could be, I'm not sure. Just didn't feel like sitting through the whole service today."

Viola picks up the newspaper and turns pages until she finds the comics. As she begins to pour her second cup, Pete Farris, hens intow, walks into The Place. Viola freezes, holding the coffee pot in one hand and the empty cup in the other.

Algie approaches the visitors. She's never met Viola's adversaries, but recognizes them by the smell of their new clothes; sugary perfumes; and the air of fresh hell that just filled the room.

"Can I help you ladies?"

Pete is standing a few inches in front of the others. Her black-and-white spectator hat, purse, and pumps are made even more spectacular as she poses on the matching checkerboard floor of The Place. She's not wearing a coat over her black wool suit with a long, mid-calf skirt.

To Pete's right is Hazel in a cream-colored coat buttoned to her neck. The wig, this week, is a jet black pageboy, placed on her head like a helmet. She keeps both hands hidden in her pockets, like a solider at attention.

Next to Hazel is Charlotte in a snow white hat with a large organza bow. Her matching white suit — pleated skirt and jacket with pleats is pleats in the back — with white tights and white patent leather boots are accented with a plain gray coat, draped over her shoulders.

To Pete's left is Deborah in blood red. As she walked through the door, she lifted the veil of her hat and folded it back over the brim. Deborah's red leather, ankle-strap sandals are not practical, but, for her, style always trumps comfort.

Peggy is beside Deborah. Her navy pea coat is unbuttoned and a white skull cap is pulled down tight over her ears, stopping at her eyelids. Her black tights are tucked snugly into her rubber boots. Unlike the others, she has not taken her eyes off Viola since they entered The Place.

Geneva is not with them.

"I'm Reverend Mrs. Henry Farris," says Pete, looking away and at everything but at Algie.

"I'm Mrs. Algie Clover. Welcome to The Place. The menu is on the chalk board. Please sit anywhere and just let me know when you're ready to order."

"We're not here to eat. We're here to speak with Viola."

The four hens stare at Viola and she returns their stares. She has put the coffee aside and is leaning against the counter with her hands on her hips.

"She's right over there Mrs. Farris. I'm sure she would be happy to speak with you. However, this is my place. So, you'll need to speak to me first."

The hens snap to attention, waiting for Pete's response.

Pete looks Algie over and steals a quick glance at Viola, who remains fixated on the hens.

"Very well, Mrs. Clover. But this matter really doesn't concern you."

"If that's the case Mrs. Farris, then you need to take your business elsewhere. Like I said, this is my place."

The hens anxiously shift their weight. Viola is immovable.

Algie's unflinching glare is undermining Pete's confidence. She decides to soften her strategy. "Perhaps Mrs. Clover, you and I could sit down and speak privately?"

"Of course, Mrs. Farris. Take a seat anywhere."

Algie asks Pete if she would like a cup of coffee.

"Yes, I think I would like a cup."

Algie motions to Viola who responds with an annoyed frown. She tightens her lips into a straight line and she shakes her head "no." Algie wets her lips and extends her pointer finger towards the front door.

Pete and the hens hold their breaths, but Viola picks up the coffee carafe and two cups and brings them to the table. She sits both cups in front of her mother, fills them, and then takes the carafe back to the hot burner.

"Sugar and cream, Mrs. Farris?"

"No, black is fine."

The two women take a couple of sips and exchange cautious glances. Algie looks directly at Pete, while the latter avoids eye contact; instead looking at Algie's forehead.

Her cup empty, Pete begins to explain the reason for her visit. "Mrs. Clover, today is a special anniversary for Mt. Moriah Missionary Baptist Church. A unique program was put together for this special occasion. And, of course, the choir was a big part of this celebration."

Algie listens and recalls Viola's clandestine solo rehearsals at the House of Faith.

"The program was going wonderfully. We had over 1200 people in attendance!"

On cue, the hens concur with a chorus of "Amen", "Praise God", and "Thank You Jesus."

Pete pauses to allow Algie the opportunity to show appreciation for this momentous milestone, too. Algie only smiles and continues to watch Pete without a word.

"As I was saying, the program was going beautifully. Everything had been planned right down to the last detail. And then, something totally unexpected and inappropriate happened! One of our finest soloists stood up to sing. Abigail, at only 18 years old, sings like she's already lived with the angels. Many people had come especially to hear her sing. The pianist began playing the opening chords of the song when, suddenly, Norma Jean and Gloria Collins rudely stepped in front of her, completely blocking her from view. In her place, Viola was at the microphone letting out the most horrible caterwauling you ever heard. No one could understand a word she was saying. And that was certainly not singing! At least, not the high standard of singing that folks have come to expect from Mt. Moriah!"

Pete angrily rises from her seat and leans towards Algie. "The rest of the choir, the pianist, the pastor, everybody was just shocked and horrified! This is the last straw, Mrs. Clover. Viola has promoted herself one time too many. And this time, in front of a full-house whose memberships will determine the destiny of Mt. Moriah. I'm here today, Mrs. Clover." Pete stops and rephrases the statement. "Rather, me and these ladies are here today, to make sure that the spiritual sanctity and integrity of Mt. Moriah are maintained and not sabotaged by someone who just wants to make a name for herself!"

Pete sits back down and hides her trembling hands beneath the table. Her face is flushed pink and her lower lip is quivering. The hens are motionless — not a flutter.

Algie watches the shaking, insecure woman sitting across from her, and realizes that Pete is scared to death of Viola. And, she should be.

"First of all, congratulations on your anniversary. It sounds like you put on a wonderful program. So, I don't understand what you think needs correcting. But, if there was a problem, it seems to me it's between you and the members of your choir. Apparently, there was a difference of opinion as to who should sing a particular song. Also, since this happened at Mt. Moriah, then Mt. Moriah is where you need to fix it, not here at The Place."

Pete quickly stands up and the hens take a step back. She turns toward Viola and shows her the deep, engraved frown that has formed on her lips and says, "Well, Sister Clover, I guess we'll see you at choir practice next week where we can discuss this matter further." Pete doesn't wait for a response. She cuts a path between the waiting hens that follow obediently.

Algie picks up the empty coffee cups and takes them to the kitchen sink. Viola finally pours herself that second cup of coffee and resumes reading the comics page.

Algie is still in the kitchen when Tressie walks down from the House of Faith to help with the Sunday dinner crowd. It's her first day back at work, since she lost Treasure.

As Tressie enters the kitchen, Algie exits with a place of collard greens and a slice of cornbread. She marvels at the contrast between her two "Christian" daughters. Tressie is faithful to her husband, her church, and her God. Viola is faithful to her wants, her needs, herself. How can her two daughters sit in churches every Sunday and walk out with two entirely different points-of-view? And yet, the non-churchgoer, Honey, is kinder and more loving than these two combined.

Maybe I'm partly to blame, Algie thinks to herself. I haven't set a very good example since Edward passed. I only attend church services on Christmas and Easter, when The Place is closed. This restaurant has become my god.

Algie scoops sliced tomatoes and raw onions over the collard greens and begins to eat, not looking at Viola. After two bites, she puts down her fork. "Viola, what are you and those bulls up to down there at that church?" Viola stretches her eyes wide, feigning surprise. "What do you mean Mama? Pete Farris and those hens are crazy! They're just a bunch of old, stuck-up, scary cows, who always think somebody is out to get them. I don't know what's wrong with them. I just pray for them."

"Viola, listen carefully, because I'm only going to say this to you once. Those women better not ever come into my place again! That means, you better not give them a reason to!"

Viola again stretches her eyeballs and starts to speak, but as she does, Algie shoves the untouched slice of cornbread into Viola's open mouth. She then picks up her plate and returns to the kitchen. Viola is laughingly spitting chunks of cornbread all over the counter.

Thirty minutes later, members of the House of Faith, including Dodd and Reverend Peters, come in for Sunday dinner. Honey is there, too. She arrived minutes before the church let out and is sitting at the far end of the counter, on the last stool. Rev. Peters takes a seat next to her. "Miss Honey, do you mind if I sit here with you?"

Honey looks into the smiling face of her sister's pastor. "Sure you can, Reverend. Have a seat. I'm not expecting anyone."

"You know, you're welcome to join us any Sunday."

"Thanks for the invite. I might take you up on that sometime."

Honey has finished her meal and pushes the plate to the side. She opens her bottle of pop and begins sipping.

Algie comes over to ask Reverend Peters what he would like for dinner. He requests the special.

"What's a pretty girl like you doing sitting here all alone?

"Alone? I'm never alone. If you're happy with yourself, you've always got company."

"Well said, Miss Honey. Well said. But don't you want a husband and children someday?"

"Sure I do. But I'm in no rush. If I can wait, so can they!"

"But, you don't want to waste your best years. That would be a crying shame."

Honey puts her pop down and looks over at Rev. Peters. She really doesn't mind talking to him, but she doesn't want this old man giving her advice about marriage and babies either.

"I'm not wasting anything Reverend. All my years will be the best. Shoot, the only thing my years need to do is try to keep up with me!"

Algie returns with Rev. Peters' dinner and shakes her head at Honey who is spinning herself around on the stool, laughing all the way. He really likes this girl. She's full of life; healthy and beautiful. Yes, he's old enough to her father, but an older man can appreciate a girl like her. He's certain that her youthful energy can be molded into a good wife and mother, and eventually, a matriarch for the church.

"But these are your prime fertile years," he continues. "This is the time in your life when you can produce the sweetest, healthiest babies."

"Is that right? Well, it seems to me I would need to find a sweet and fertile husband before I go barking up that tree."

He watches Honey sipping her pop and asks, "How many dates will it take before I can shake that tree?"

Honey drops her pop on the lunch counter. She has to use both hands to grab the runaway bottle. Once the bottle is again upright, she throws her head back in uncontrollable laughter. Soon, tears are seeping from Honey's tightly closed eyes and she's gulping for air. Customers sitting in the restaurant begin smiling and nodding toward Honey and Rev. Peters, assuming the pair is sharing a very funny joke.

Rev. Peters is too embarrassed to move from his seat. He stares down at his food with a forced smile.

Finally, Honey regains her composure. She gently and apologetically pats his arm. She didn't mean to hurt his feelings, but the thought of her being with him was deliciously funny.

Slowly, Rev. Peters stands up. He thanks her for her time and leaves his uneaten dinner on the counter. He acknowledges a nod from two of his parishioners as he walks out the front door, the sting of her laughing rejection burning in his ears.

Algie asked Mazy to be at The Place next Thursday. The two women have decided that there still is no good reason to tell Viola anything.

On Thursday, Viola, as usual, is sitting at the counter drinking coffee. As planned, Mazy comes to The Place and Algie introduces her to Tressie and Viola as an old friend from Dublin. Tressie responds enthusiastically. She asks Mazy how things are going in Dublin and how she is adjusting to life up north. Viola, on the other hand, says hello, but nothing else. Mazy tries to engage by complementing her hairstyle, her choir robe, and even her singing voice. Mazy had been at the Mt. Moriah celebration when Viola sang her solo. Viola responds to each inquiry with a short "thank you". She never looks at Mazy.

Algie had suggested to Mazy that a barrage of compliments might appeal to Viola's vanity, but it isn't working. Mazy is now asking Viola if she has a special fellow.

"What do you mean a special fellow? I don't need no man to make me feel special."

Hurt by the rebuke, May gives up. She had hoped there would be some naturalness between them that would allow for a friendship, but this first attempt has failed.

"Viola, there's no reason to be so nasty," says Algie. "Mazy is a dear friend from home who is just trying to get to know you better. She doesn't mean you any harm."

"She asks too many questions," says Viola, talking as if Mazy weren't in the room.

"It's the questions we don't ask ourselves that are the hardest to answer," replies Algie, giving Viola a look so hard that even Mazy feels the weight of it.

She had hoped to visit longer, but Mazy says her good-byes and prepares to leave after only 15 minutes. Tressie hugs her warmly. Algie's hug follows. Viola never turns around.

Not long after Mazy' departure, the sound of a police siren gets louder and louder. Algie expects the emergency vehicle to zoom down Germantown, past The Place, but it doesn't. The police cruiser and ambulance stop right in front of the restaurant.

Everyone inside The Place is peering out the windows. Algie goes outside. The cops are next door at Crook's. She recognizes one of the cabbies and motions for him to come over.

"What's going on? Where's Crook?"

The cabbie doesn't know. "Something happened out back, Miss Algie. Somebody got mad and pulled out a knife. One man is laying in the alley bleeding. Crook was trying to get him up before the cops came. I don't know who done the stabbing."

The ambulance attendants bring the injured man out on a gurney and load him into the ambulance. The police are interviewing Crook's customers.

One of the cops approaches Algie, and the cabbie quickly walks away and merges into the crowd standing in front of Clover's.

"Evening. Are you Algie Clover?"

"Yes, I am."

"I was told you're related to Willie Clover, the guy that runs this poolroom. Is that correct?"

"Yes and no. Willie is my late husband's cousin, but he's no relation to me."

The officer smiles. "I understand Mrs. Clover. Well, we've been getting reports of some bad things going on in the alley behind this poolroom. Did you see or hear anything unusual this evening?"

"No, I didn't. I was busy in my restaurant. I didn't hear anything."

"Do you ever go out into the alley?"

"The only time I go into the alley is to take out the trash."

"When you take out the trash, who do you see in the alley? Do you speak to anyone? Do they say anything to you?"

"No, I don't see or speak to anyone back there. When I take the trash out, it's dark. The can is right by the door, so I can see it from the light in the kitchen. It takes me less than a minute. I don't see nobody and I don't hear nothing."

The cop considers her answers. Clearly, she and the owner of the game room don't get along. He won't press her now, but she probably knows more than she's letting on. "Well, thank you for your time Mrs. Clover. If you think of anything else, give us a call."

The policeman walks back over to Crook's. Algie stays on the sidewalk for a few minutes longer, watching the cops conduct their investigation. She then re-enters The Place.

"What's happening over at Uncle Crook's?"

"Not sure, but, somebody got stabbed out back in the alley."

Tressie screams. "Was it Uncle Crook?"

"No, no it wasn't Crook. But he is missing. He's probably lying low somewhere until things quiet down. Let's get back to work."

The customers return to their meals, and Algie takes her seat. She doesn't wish bad on nobody, but Crook is certainly reaping what he's sown. Maybe he did the stabbing. If he did, that should keep him gone a long while, maybe for good.

The next day, Clover's Pool Room is closed. Several of his customers come to The Place inquiring about Crook. It did seem odd, though, for Clover's to be closed. Algie and Tressie both feel the awkwardness. At first, Algie enjoyed the quiet, but soon she missed the noises and customers that came from next door.

Crook's disappearance is the "talk" on Dayton's Westside. Benny has been discussing it with nearly every customer that has come into his bar. From his patrons, he's learned enough information to piece together the rumors and gossip into a plausible story. During his lunch break at The Place, he tells Algie and Tressie what he's heard.

A fight broke out in the alley. A guy named Oscar accused a man of cheating, which was true. Oscar tried to get his money back, but the man wouldn't budge. At first it was just fists, and Crook tried to break them up and settle the argument. Next thing anybody remembers, the accused man pulled out a knife. He cut Oscar pretty bad and the ambulance had to take him. He's still in Miami Valley Hospital.

The man who attacked him ran, but the cops found him at his mother's house and arrested him. Nobody knows where Crook is hiding. The police want him for illegal gambling and selling liquor without a license.

It's been two months since the telegram came and Early still has not returned from Texas. Algie decides to write to him. She's written enough letters for him and has memorized his mother's address.

Algie is not the only one concerned about Early's delayed return.

Tressie told her that Screamie's mother recently came by The Place. She wanted to know if anyone had heard from him. Tressie offered to call Algie who was at the house, but the woman declined.

Business is slow that evening, so Algie decides to close early. Tressie calls Dodd, and while she waits, helps Algie clean. After Tressie and Dodd pull away from the curb, Algie catches sight of the witch. She snatches her coat from the rack and races out the front door. She is walking several steps behind, all the while silently praying that she doesn't stop at her doorway. The witch paces herself, walking slowly but deliberately along Germantown. If she knows Algie is behind her, she acts as if she doesn't. She turns right on Fitch Street and Algie feels her heart pounding. She prays in a low whisper, "Lord, please don't let her stop at my house."

The witch keeps going, past Dunbar.

Algie stands on the corner and watches her until she disappears. When she gets to her house, Algie doesn't immediately go in. She takes a seat on the porch. The dispatcher's stand is dark and there is no sound coming from the parked cabs. She looks up and sees an array of stars in the sky. They look the way she feels right now — lost and stranded.

Bo comes by the house regularly. He spends several evenings on the couch with Honey, watching the new television. Chauncey won't admit it, but she likes him. Bo always speaks to her when he comes and she's not forgotten how nice he was to her the day she tried to go back to Georgia. The TV has also brought Algie peace of mind in an unexpected way. Now, when she checks on Chauncey, she finds her hypnotized by the TV.

Chauncey doesn't change the channel because she's afraid of breaking it. She watches whatever program comes on. Even when

Viola darkens the door, Chauncey now ignores her and focuses on whoever is talking on the television.

Since the stabbing at the poolroom, Benny now walks Algie home at nights. He leaves his two waitress in-charge and accompanies Algie home every night, except Sundays when his bar is closed. Like their restaurant conversations, it's mostly small talk. He's careful not to say anything negative about Early, but he's asked about the latter's whereabouts a couple of times. Algie either doesn't know or won't tell him. Then, finally, she mentions to him that she wrote Early a letter, sending it to his mother's address in Sweetwater. Ever cautious, Benny lets the new information sink in before responding.

"Well, that's good. Now we can just hope against hope that he will get in touch with you, to let you know what's going on."

Algie looks at him incredulously. "Hope against hope? Why would anybody hope against hope?"

SEVEN

Ruby runs into The Place, panting. "Honey here, Miss Algie?"

"No, she isn't. Sit down Ruby before you fall down. What's got you running?"

Ruby drops into the nearest chair. Algie goes into the kitchen and returns with a cup of water. "Here, drink this down. Catch your breath so you can tell me what's wrong with you."

Ruby empties the cup and takes a deep breath. "Miss Algie, you won't believe what just happened over at Mt. Moriah. I was just dropping my mother off for choir practice. When we got there, there was a huge crowd outside on the front lawn."

"What happened? Was someone hurt?"

"No, ma'am. It was a fight!"

"A fight! Who in the world was fighting in front of a church?"

"Miss Algie it was the hens and the bulls. Norma Jean and Gloria Collins were on one side and Pete and her crew was on the other. Miss Algie, Miss Algie. You should have seen it.

"Wigs flying, shoes everywhere, hats rolling across the grass, purses open and stuff spilling everywhere. When me and my mother pulled up, Norma Jean had Pete face down on the ground with her knee in Pete's back. Deborah James and Peggy Linwood were trying to help Pete, but they weren't being too successful because Deborah's blouse was pulled wide open and Peggy had two large holes in the knees of her stockings. Big old Norma Jean was handling them both! Pete was eating dirt and all Deborah and Peggy could do was hold on, they couldn't move Norma Jean an inch.

"Hazel Fuqua was running around in circles crying and trying to get her wig back on her head. I looked over on the side of the church and Charlotte Milton was in a hair pulling contest with Gloria, and losing. Gloria was yanking Charlotte up-and-down and from side-to-side like a rag doll. Geneva Black was on all fours turning around in circles grabbing at the air, but catching nothing.

"Miss Algie, it was a holy mess! I have never seen anything like it. My mother was just outdone. She wouldn't even get out of the car. The other members of the choir were just standing around staring. I think they just didn't know what to do."

Algie was reluctant to ask, but she had to know. "Ruby, was Viola in it?"

Ruby pauses to think for a moment. "No, no, Miss Algie, I didn't see her there."

Hmmm. Something's not right about that, Algie thinks to herself.

"Well, who broke it up?"

"They all just kind of stopped on their own. Norma Jean finally let Pete get back up. Gloria dropped Charlotte to the ground and let go of her hair.

"Then, Pete and her women went hollering, screaming, and running as fast and hard as they could around to the back of the church. Norma Jean and Gloria didn't chase after them. They took their time straightening out their clothes and wiping themselves off as best they could. I don't need to tell you, that was the end of choir rehearsal. I took my mama back home and came right over here."

"What a mess, Ruby. Honey is around to the house if you still want to go and see her. I guess I need to track down Viola to make sure she's alright."

Algie has no idea where to look for Viola. She considers calling the pastor at Mt. Moriah, but dismisses the idea. Viola will show, sooner or later. It turned out to be much later.

There was evidence that she'd been at the house, but not while Algie was there and only when Chauncey was napping. Algie left a note on the bed asking Viola to come by The Place, but for three days, she stayed away.

When she finally did come back, Viola refused to discuss the brawl at the church, while loudly proclaiming her innocence.

The following Saturday, the postman brings a letter from Texas. Algie immediately recognizes the familiar scrawl on the enclosed note. Early's mother scribbled two, short sentences: Early got killed. Buried him next to his daddy. There was no salutation and no closing signature.

Killed.

Algie thinks of the telegram that didn't make any sense but sent Early back to Texas: "Cracker's in the soup, come stir the pot." She hadn't read those actual words back to Early. Instead, she told him there was a family emergency. After all, his mother had sent a telegram. She had assumed the message was some kind of code.

When Benny came for dinner that evening, he saw the letter from Texas on the counter. He didn't ask about it. Instead, he waited until Algie was busy with a customer and motioned for Tressie to come over. Benny kept his eyes on Algie and silently mouthed his question. "What was in the letter?" Tressie glances over at her mother and in a hoarse whisper says, "Dead and buried!" She then goes back to the kitchen.

Dead and buried?

It took a moment for Benny to absorb Tressie's words. Yes, he wanted Early out of the way, but he didn't wish the man dead! What could have happened? He had assumed Early had decided to stay in Texas. He figured that do-nothing would live-off his mother and excuse himself from any further responsibility to his daughter, Screamie.

Benny can't believe it. What did that fool get himself into back in Texas?

When Algie returns to her stool, she notices the troubled look on Benny's face. She asks him twice "what's wrong?" She repeats herself for a third time. "Hello? Benny? I said what's wrong? You look like somebody just stole your last dollar!" Algie laughs as he rapidly blinks his eyes, trying to wake from his daydream. "Sorry Algie, I wasn't ignoring you, just got a little lost in my thoughts."

"What's on your mind? You're not having any problems with the bar, are you?"

"No, everything's fine. I was just daydreaming a little, but it's nothing to worry about."

Benny finishes his dinner and heads back across the street. He'll be back to walk Algie home.

Algie didn't cry for Early, but she felt a tinge of pain when she'd hear a voice that sounded his or catch a glimpse of a passerby with a similar profile. Worst of all, was looking over at the place where Screamie's mat used to be.

As Tressie and Algie are sitting at a table waiting to leave — the former for Dodd, the latter for Benny — Algie gets up to answer the knock at the locked and closed door. She is surprised to see Honey, followed by Viola.

Viola plops her oversized bible on the counter. Honey takes a seat next to Tressie who says, "We just closed, what brings your frowning faces in here this late?"

Viola ignores the question, Honey pouts.

"We're headed home so you both will be going out the door, just as quickly as you came in," says Algie. "But, Viola since you're here, I still want to know who or what caused that big fight at Mt. Moriah's. I've warned you; I want no uninvited guests in this restaurant again?"

"Yes," says Honey. "Ruby told me her version, what's yours?"

Algie ignores Viola's silence and continues her questioning. "Where were you when all this was going on? You and those Collins sisters are inseparable. How's it that you missed the fight?"

Tressie and Honey stare at Viola, eagerly awaiting her reply.

Viola turns her back to Algie and her sisters. "I wasn't there and I didn't have anything to do it."

"Whether you were there or not," says Tressie. "You had something to do with it. Of that, I'm sure. Like mama said, everyone knows how close you and those bulls are; some people say a little too close."

"I didn't have anything to do with it."

Tressie rolls her eyes and snaps her finger. "You had something to do with it. But you slid away, just in time, to let others finish the mess you started."

"What in the Sam hell do you know about it Tressie? You weren't there! And, you don't know nothing about my private business."

"Private business? Everyone in this family knows exactly what your business is, who you doing your business with, and how you covering your business up with visits from that witch."

Viola throws her Bible at Tressie, just missing the latter's head. Honey jumps to her feet. Algie is too angry to speak.

"Viola, have you lost your mind? Just who do you think you are?"

Viola backs up like a bull, kicking her heels behind her. Honey is equally as furious, she steps in front of Algie, spitting curses at Viola.

Tressie puts up her hand to stop Honey. "Stay back. Let me handle this! Then, turning towards Viola, she adds, "look you satin doll whore, wrapped in a choir robe, don't you ever throw anything at me! Maybe you got them bulls fooled, but I know Rev. Farris ain't the only man spending time up under that robe."

Algie steps around Honey and takes a position between Tressie and Viola. "All three of you take a seat!" Honey quickly complies, but not her sisters.

Viola rips off her choir robe and throws it on the floor. As her eyes narrow like zippers, she leans forward, ready to charge.

"Say what you got to say, Tressie. But you better be ready to back it up!"

Viola leaps, bringing her clenched fists down on Tressie's face. As Tressie's stunned body slumps to the floor, Algie picks up the robe and swings it at Viola, blinding her and sending her to the floor alongside Tressie.

Dodd saw Algie leaving, but couldn't catch her attention as he was parking. He walks into The Place and immediately takes a step backwards. Viola is on the floor; curled into a fetal position, staring into space, and tangled up in her choir robe. Honey is stroking her hair and Tressie is standing over both of them, her hands folded in prayer.

"What has happened? Is Viola sick?"

Honey shakes her head "no" and begins trying to lift Viola from the floor.

Dodd hurries over to help Honey and places the choir robe over Viola's shoulders and again asks, "Are you sick? Was Miss Algie going for help?"

Tressie doesn't help them. She walks outside and Dodd soon follows, bumping into Benny who has come to take Algie home. Dodd tells him what he found inside and that Algie has already left. As they drive away, he and Tressie watch Honey and Benny leading Viola by the hand, out the door and onto the sidewalk. Dodd wants to stop and offer them a ride to Dunbar, but Tressie waves him on.

The year comes to an end and a new decade will begin. It's

December 31, 1959. Everyone living on the west side is in turmoil over the marches and protests going on in the South. Some are torn between staying or going back home to help bring about change.

Algie and her daughters feel the movement in the air, too. But Dayton is now their home. Tressie is pregnant again. Honey and Bo eloped in September. Viola is still waging war, alongside the bulls, against Pete and the hens. And, Clover's Pool Room is now called George's Place, and the former cabbie is still ordering his lunch from The Place.

Algie and Benny are beginning the New Year as a couple. He's taking her to dinner across the street at Flamingo's. It's the first time she has ever gone on a date.

Predictably, Chauncey did not approve of the relationship. But when Benny purchased a used TV for Algie, since Honey and Bo took the new one with them when they got married, Chauncey has said nothing more about his frequent visits.

Sitting on her front porch, waiting for Benny, Algie tries to count the stars as they come out. The air is cold, but she's warm inside. A train is whistling, probably headed down South. On the cab lot, the glow from a single cigarette flickers like a lightning bug as the dispatcher settles in for a long night. Algie patiently waits for the familiar memories of Dublin, but they don't come. She again looks into the night sky. Even the stars look new as they sparkle their way into the New Year.

ABOUT THE AUTHOR

Sharon KD Hoskins has worked in the field of communications for more than 20 years. She has a B.A. in mass communication arts (Hampton University) and a M.P.H. in public health practice (University of South Florida). Her first novel, *To Handcuff Lightning*, is an "Eric Hoffer Award finalist". All of her stories are told with humor, candor, and the belief that love will eventually show up. She is a member of the Atlanta Writers Club and enjoys reading historical fiction, contemporary humor, and mysteries solved by a cat.

www.ingramcontent.com/pod-product-compliance
Lightning Source LLC
Chambersburg PA
CBHW070343130626
46556CB00007B/3004